THE SECRET

A SINGLE IN SEATTLE NOVEL

KRISTEN PROBY

AMPERSAND PUBLISHING, INC.

The Secret
A Single in Seattle Novel
By
Kristen Proby

This one is for you.

PROLOGUE

~OLIVIA~

Ten Years Ago

"*D*ad, I want to go with you."

I'm sitting on my parents' bed, watching as my father packs his suitcase. Mom already did hers. She packs *way* in advance, but Dad's always doing it at the last minute.

I think it secretly makes my mom want to pull her hair out, and that's saying a lot since my parents still act like newlyweds, even after being married for fifteen years.

It's kind of gross.

"We've been over this," he says as he tosses a pair of jeans into his suitcase. "You and your brother and sisters are staying with Nanny and Pap."

I roll my eyes and sigh heavily. "I'm not a baby anymore, you know. I'm *fifteen* and definitely old enough to go to the Oscars. What if you *win*? I want to be there. I want to celebrate with you."

"And you will, *after* your mom and I get home. We always have a big party afterwards with the whole family."

"It's not the same." I frown down at my pink Chuck Taylors. "You know, being famous isn't that bad of a thing. It's actually really cool, but you make it sound like it's the end of the world. If you hate it so much, why do you still do it? It's hypocritical and stupid."

His head comes up. His eyes narrow on me, and I know I just took it too far.

He definitely won't let me go now.

"I've worked my ass off to balance the scales of fame and family, Olivia Williams, and I'll be damned if I listen to my teenager berate me for it because she's throwing a little fit."

"I shouldn't have said that; I know. But, Dad—"

"No. You shouldn't have said that."

His voice is hard, and I know I've royally pissed him off and ruined any chance I might have had of talking him into letting me go.

Not that the chance was high to begin with, but I like to think it was better than zero.

"I'm sorry." I reach for his hand when he moves to walk away. "I really am, Daddy. You're kind of a nerd, but you're also totally cool."

"Nerd, am I?" His face softens just a little, and I know he won't be mad at me for long. He never is.

"Have you seen the action figures in your office? None of us kids play with toys anymore."

"I caught Keaton in there checking them out just last week."

"He's a nerd, too." I smile up at him. "Dad, why do you hate it so much? Why are you so strict about protecting us from Hollywood?"

He sighs and sits next to me, leaning over to kiss my forehead.

"I hate the internet," he mutters and rubs his hand down his face. "Because being famous isn't all fun parties and big houses, Liv. The press is a bitch. We'll have this talk later. But for now, if I don't finish packing, your mother will have my hide, and I make it a point not to piss her off."

"And yet, you always wait until the last minute to pack."

He stops and frowns down at me. "Whose side are you on, anyway, little girl?"

I laugh and shake my head. "Whichever one keeps me out of trouble."

"BEST DIRECTOR IS UP NEXT!" Keaton announces as Nanny hurries back into the room with fresh popcorn for us all. "He's gonna win. He's *totally* gonna win!"

3

"It takes forever," Haley complains with a pout. "Why are the Oscars so *long*?"

"Because they have a lot of people to honor," Pap says with a wink. "A lot of work goes into movies."

Dad's movie did well this year. Several from his production company were nominated, but the one he directed and produced totally cleaned up. Best actor, best actress, and best costume design, just for starters. Every time the camera pans over to him, Dad's full of proud smiles.

Dang it, I wish I was there.

We all hold our breath as they announce the nominees. Chelsea, being the youngest at ten, clutches my hand with all her might.

"Come on, come on, come on," she whispers.

"And the Oscar goes to…Luke Williams!"

"Yes!"

"Yay!"

"I knew it!"

As we watch Dad kiss our mom and then walk up on stage, we all clap and jump up and down with excitement.

"Hush, now. He's speaking," Nan says.

"What an honor," Dad begins and then smiles down at Mom in that goofy way he always does. "Wow. Well, first, of course, I have to thank my gorgeous wife for loving me and putting up with a *lot*. Same goes for my kids, who are all watching from home with my parents, who are also just the best. I love you guys."

"I love you, too," Haley says to the TV as Gran wipes away tears.

He goes on to thank his crew, the actors, and the other people that he works with. Many names are familiar because I eavesdrop all the time on my dad's conversations.

"Thank you very much. Thank you for watching movies. We love bringing them to you."

And with that, he holds his gold statue up and then walks off the stage.

Among the applause in the audience, the camera pans down to the actors, all smiling and clapping.

Suddenly, I catch a glimpse of Christian Wolfe, one of my parents' friends, who I've had a crush on since *forever*. He's just the *ultimate.*

I grin over at Chelsea. "I'm totally gonna marry a movie star."

CHAPTER 1

~OLIVIA~

"*I* freaking *hate* movie stars," I declare as I sit across from Stella and Erin. These two are my family. Well, two of about sixty others, but two of the closest.

Stella's mom and mine are best friends and pretty much sisters. So, Stella and I have been attached at the hip since she came out of the womb less than a year after me.

And Erin is a few years younger, but this family of cousins is *close.* I live with these two, along with our other cousin, Drew.

"So, you're saying you need a drink," Stella says with a smile as the waitress approaches. Stella points to her martini glass full of what looks to be a dirty martini. "She needs one of these."

"I need food, too," I add. "A cheeseburger and fries, please."

"Me, too," Erin says.

"Make it three," Stella says with a nod and then turns back to me. "Okay, so why do you hate movie stars *today*?"

"So rude," I grumble and steal a sip of her martini while waiting for mine. "I had an appointment today for a fitting with Vaughn Barrymore, and he stood me up. Didn't even bother to call. Or have his assistant call, anyway. I'm so damn busy, you guys. The costumes for this movie are intricate and take hundreds of hours to make, and now I'm behind because the star of the film didn't have the decency to make it into my office on time. Or, you know, at all."

"He's hot," Erin declares and earns a glare from me. She then smiles innocently. "I mean, in a total douchebag kind of way, of course. But have you seen his dimples?"

"Which ones?" Stella asks with a smirk. "Because in that one movie he did last year, we got to see his ass, and the dimples above those cheeks are also pretty fantastic. Wait, I wonder if that was an ass double."

"I hear he does his own stunts," I say and can't help but laugh with them. "And let me just say, a guy can be the hottest thing ever and *not* be nice. So the looks don't matter."

"They don't hurt," Stella says and then holds up her perfectly manicured hands in surrender when I narrow my eyes at her. "Okay, you're right. If he's an asshat, he's not hot."

"I know that a lot of people don't take me seriously because I work at my dad's production company," I continue after the waitress delivers my drink. I immediately eat the blue-cheese-stuffed olive that came in it. "They think that I only got the job of lead costume designer because I'm his kid, but damn it, I worked my ass off for *years* to get this job. I got it on my own."

"Absolutely," Erin agrees. "We hardly saw you for years while you were in school and then in apprenticeships. You're always behind a sewing machine. Covered in fabric. How you have that tan, I'll never know."

"Sometimes, she hauls the sewing machine outside," Stella says, and I sip my martini, watching them.

"I go outside," I reply dryly. "Sitting by the pool is my favorite hobby. Next to making clothes, anyway. I *like* my job, you guys. I love it. But I hate the part where I have to interact with celebrities. My dad was right: Famous people aren't all they're cracked up to be."

"We already knew that," Stella reminds me. "Half our family is famous, and they're great, but they're just normal people. And half the people they work with are idiots."

"My dad is a total weirdo," Erin supplies, and I smile at the thought of her father, former football star, Will Montgomery.

Women still send him fan mail that his daughters love to read and tease him about. It's really pretty hilarious.

"Your dad is funny," I say, shaking my head. "And

considerate. I'm pretty sure that if he ever had to have a fitting, he'd show up for it."

"True. He would." Erin sighs and then grins when our burgers are delivered. "I'm gonna need to run ten miles to burn off this burger, and I don't even care."

"It's girls' night, so it doesn't count," Stella says and takes a big bite.

"If it were a *true* girls' night, we would have invited the other cousins," I point out. "But, since we're all girls, and we're together, it counts. Erin, how's it going with that sports reporter you've been dating?"

The light goes out of her pretty blue eyes, and I immediately apologize. "I'm sorry, did I miss something?"

"He's also an asshat," Erin says with a shrug. "I like that word. He just wanted to hang out with my dad, who had no interest in hanging out with *him*, and we never got to a third date. Thank God. I'm so glad I adopted my mom's three-date rule because I would have been really pissed if I'd slept with him."

"How does that work again?" Stella wants to know.

"You don't have sex until *after* the third date," Erin says. "That way, you know when the dude is just in it to get in your pants."

"What if you *want* him in your pants?" Stella wonders.

"I'm telling you, three dates is the rule," Erin insists. "By then, the ones who are in it for the right reasons are still around."

"Erin," I say softly and reach over to pat her hand. "Are you a...*virgin?*"

"No." She laughs, and her cheeks darken. Which happens a lot when you have gorgeous red hair. "I'm not. But I also don't sleep with every date because that's just gross."

"Three dates can be a long time," Stella says and brushes her long, blonde hair over her shoulder. "What if you can only see each other once a week because you're super busy? You're going to wait three weeks?"

"Four," Erin says and pops a fry into her mouth. "Because it has to be *after* the third date."

I press my lips together to hold in laughter as Stella just blinks at our cousin in disbelief. "Like, a *month?*"

"I guess Stella doesn't abide by the three-date rule," I say with a laugh and sip my martini. This is exactly what I needed tonight after the shitshow of a day I just finished. Some time to blow off steam with my girls. Some laughs.

I'll worry about Vaughn Barrymore tomorrow.

"WHERE WERE YOU GUYS?" Drew asks when the three of us walk into the house several hours later, laughing. He's in the kitchen, as usual, munching on leftover pizza.

Drew's also a cousin and lives in the guest house out back, where my mom's studio used to be. But he eats in here and spends most of his time inside when he's home.

"We met up after work," I inform him. "How was your day?"

"Fine." He licks his fingers and then starts to reach into the cookie jar.

"Michael Andrew Montgomery, don't you *dare.*"

He stops cold at the scolding from Erin and blinks innocently. "No one calls me by my real name but my mom. And only when I'm in trouble."

"Touch those cookies with your spit-covered fingers, and you'll be in trouble," I advise. "That's just disgusting."

"Living with girls is so—"

"Say '*annoying*,' and you can go live with your mom," I say with a sweet smile. "How is Brynna, anyway?"

"Great. Better if I don't live with her and Dad." He laughs and washes his hands, then pulls three peanut butter cookies out of the jar. "I might have a guest over this weekend. Just giving you a heads-up." He winks suggestively, and I wrinkle my nose at him.

Stella raises an eyebrow. "Who's the lucky girl?"

"You don't know her." He finishes off one cookie and starts on the next. "I just met her today. The woman has legs a mile long."

"I don't think Drew abides by the three-date rule, either," Erin mutters. "I'm going to bed. Goodnight, guys."

She hurries up the stairs, and when we hear her

door close softly, Drew looks between Stella and me. "What did I say?"

"She's not dating the sports reporter anymore," Stella informs him. "He was an asshole and just using her because of who her dad is."

"He's a *sports reporter*," Drew says, as if that explains everything. "Her dad is one of the most famous football players of all time. Did she think he didn't have ulterior motives? Of course, he was a jerk. But it's not my place to say that. I'll buy her ice cream tomorrow. Cherry Garcia usually makes her feel better."

"You know, you try to make everyone think you're a tough guy, but deep down, you're a softie."

Drew narrows his eyes at me, chewing the last cookie. "Take it back."

"Nope. Softie."

Finally, he just shrugs. "Erin's sweet. She doesn't deserve a jerk like that guy. Anyway, how are you two?"

"Fine—"

"Good," Stella and I say at the same time.

"Okay, well, that was a stimulating conversation. I'm going to bed. Later." He waves and walks out the back door toward the guesthouse.

"I like him," I say to Stella as we turn to the stairs. "He's not nearly as annoying as he was when he was a kid."

"Only sometimes," she replies.

"THIS IS A BIG PROJECT," Dad says from across his desk. We have a standing meeting every Thursday morning at ten to go over everything I've been assigned. I don't think he does this with any of the other employees. He just likes to see me.

And I like it, too, so I'm not complaining.

"My biggest to-date," I confirm.

"No pressure here, Liv, but this could garner Oscar attention."

I don't flinch as I hold his blue gaze with mine. "I know. And, yes, I'm young, but I can do this. I have an amazing staff who knows what they're doing. The designs are *stunning*—even if I'm the one who designed them. Yes, it could definitely get recognized this year. If it turns out the way I think it will, it *should* be."

"And that doesn't make you nervous?"

I shake my head slowly. "No. It's my job, Mr. Williams."

His lips twitch with humor. I refuse to call him *Dad* when I'm at work. I also use my mother's maiden name professionally, not because I'm not proud to be my father's daughter, but because I want to be recognized for my talent, not my name.

And Dad understood when I told him so.

"You're right. The sketches of the designs are great. It's going to be a visually stunning film. Any hang-ups yet?"

"Only your star."

His eyes narrow now. "How so?"

I explain about Vaughn missing our appointment yesterday.

"If I can't get his measurements down to the millimeter, I can't make the costumes, and he'll play the part naked."

"Well, that would be interesting, wouldn't it? I'm sure it was a scheduling snafu. Have your assistant reach out to his."

"Already done," I say with a sigh. "We have most of the other measurements already, and my staff has begun sewing. The budget on this is high. Like, scary expensive. These fabrics aren't cheap."

"Nothing on this film is cheap," he replies easily. "It never is. I don't see any issues with the budget you've proposed here. Filming begins in three months, and we'll need the costumes a month before that."

"That's not a problem." It'll be tight, but we'll be done in time. "Now, let's talk about the romcom I'll be working on next month."

"Liv, I think that's a lot on your plate."

I blink up at him. "Excuse me?"

"Two projects at once is a lot for anyone. I don't expect my directors, actors, sound techs, or anyone else to juggle two projects. They do one at a time."

"I can handle it."

He shakes his head, but I dig in my heels.

"It's not like I have a crazy social life over here, Mr. Williams. I can handle the extra work."

"Maybe you *should* have a crazy social life," he

suggests. "You're twenty-five and already a workaholic."

"I learned from the best." I wink at him, and his face softens. "I can take on the romcom. It's not nearly as technical as the other project, and I won't be sewing the majority of the costumes. It's all designer clothes. So, although it's easier on *me*, it's not easier on the budget."

"Never is," he repeats. "Okay, show me what you've got."

We spend another thirty minutes going over costume plans before I stand to leave.

"You're doing an excellent job."

I grin at him. "Thanks, boss. I'll see you this weekend for dinner."

He winks, and I leave his office, walking down the hall to the elevator and then heading down to my floor. We use the entire floor for costumes—and not just for *my* movies. We have several sewing rooms, a large area designated for climate-controlled storage, places for display, and fitting rooms where actors can try on costumes. It takes a lot of space to make sure the clothes are just right.

My office is in the corner with a view of Seattle. I have plenty of space to do private fittings and measurements in here, which I appreciate because running back and forth to the other fitting areas can eat up a bunch of time, and this is convenient.

I walk through the door to my office and come to an abrupt stop.

Sitting *on my freaking desk*, his feet dangling, is Vaughn Barrymore. He scowls when he sees me in the doorway.

"You know, you could have let me know that you were going to be late," he says.

I blink, walk inside, and shut the door, setting the folders and papers in my arms on a shelf before propping my hands on my hips.

"I'm Olivia Conner. I'll be working with you. Of course, our appointment was scheduled for *yesterday,* and you didn't call to reschedule, but I'll make room in *my* busy schedule to fit you in. You're welcome."

That scowl doesn't leave his too-handsome-for-his-own-good face. "We did not have an appointment yesterday. It's today."

"Yesterday," I repeat and reach for my measuring tape, trying to ignore the fact that Vaughn might be sexier in person than he is in the movies. "But we can knock it out right now before my next appointment. It won't take long. Just stand over here."

Vaughn hops off the desk and stands in the middle of the room. I squat before him, tape in hand to measure his inseam, then frown.

"You're wearing jeans."

"Smart one, aren't you?"

I raise my eyebrows and stare up at him. God, he *is* hotter in person. That's just not fair.

Get it together, Liv. You're a professional.

"I asked you to wear sweats or something loose so I could get an accurate measurement. It's important."

Without a word, Vaughn takes off his shoes, unfastens his jeans, lets them drop to pool around his feet, then steps out of them and flicks them aside with his toe.

Thank God he's wearing underwear.

I mean, it's tight-as-hell boxer briefs and leaves absolutely *nothing* to the imagination, but he's covered.

Sort of.

And holy Jesus in Heaven, the man is *hung.* How am I going to get this measurement without making a fool of myself?

"Better?"

"Sure. Just…spread your legs a bit."

He grins and obliges.

"This isn't so bad, after all," he says, and I snarl at him.

He's warm and so freaking *firm* as I measure from his crotch to his ankle and then quickly move to his waist, turning to jot down the numbers.

I have to measure each thigh and calf, and then, finally, I can stand before him and out of range of *that.*

God, I'm flushed. Sure, Vaughn's potent on screen, but he's no less so in person. Maybe even *sexier* in person. I wasn't expecting that.

He's also cocky and rude.

"Please raise your arms like this." I lift mine straight out from my sides, and he mimics me. "Perfect."

I have to wrap my arms around him, like in a hug, to grab the tape and pull it around his chest. When I lean in, I swear I hear him take a deep breath through his nose, near my head.

"Did you just *sniff* me?" I demand after jerking back.

His lips—his *full* and gorgeous lips—twist into a sneer. "In your dreams, sweetheart."

"Unlike every other woman in this country, I don't dream about you."

"Try the *world*."

"God, you're so full of yourself," I mutter under my breath and make a note of the chest measurement.

"What did you just say?"

I sigh and turn back to him. "I said I have to get something off my shelf."

"No, that's definitely *not* what you said."

"Okay." I prop my hands on my hips and square my shoulders. This guy doesn't intimidate me. "I said that you're full of yourself."

"What the hell is that supposed to mean?"

"Aww, poor Vaughn. I'm not fawning all over you. I bet you're not used to a woman with a backbone, are you?"

"You have a mouth on you, don't you?"

You have no idea.

"Look, we're done here." I turn away and try *not* to think about how warm he is or how good he smells.

19

How firm his damn body is.

Why does he have to be a jerk?

"Great."

And with that, he pulls on his pants and hurries out of my office.

Thankfully, aside from a couple of fittings, I won't have to deal with Vaughn Barrymore often.

And then I glance down at my paper and realize that I forgot to do his shoulders and neck.

Damn it!

I run out of my office and find him waiting by the elevators.

"Vaughn," I call out, and his face whips up, his gaze meeting mine.

His green eyes look...*frustrated.*

"I need a couple more measurements."

"I thought you said we were done."

"I was wrong." I swallow hard. "I apologize. I need just a few more minutes of your time."

He rubs his hand over his mouth and then nods curtly before marching ahead of me and back into my office.

I close the door behind me and reach for my tape.

"I just need your arms, shoulders, and neck. I'll start with your shoulders."

I briskly and professionally measure Vaughn's broad shoulders, down his arms, and then his wrists, all from behind.

Which is a relief because he can't see the flush on my cheeks. Why is he so...*sexy?*

I take my notes and quickly measure his neck.

Before I can back away, Vaughn spins around, grips my hair in a fist, and plants his lips on mine in a kiss that makes my knees turn to jelly.

Holy shit, the man can *kiss.* But I push back and breathlessly ask, "Why did you do that?"

His green eyes shine with lust, but they haven't lost their look of frustration.

"Because you're sexy, and I might have lost my head for a minute."

I narrow my eyes. "I don't like you."

"I don't like you, either."

"Great." I jump on him, frame his face in my palms, and give as good as I just got. His hands move to my ass, holding me against him as we plunder each other's mouths and kiss as if it's our last dying wish. As if we couldn't stop if we wanted to.

And I *don't* want to.

He spins and lowers me to my desk, and my senses return.

"Hold up." I press a hand to his chest, and he stops immediately.

"What's wrong? I'm sorry, I thought you were okay with this—"

"I'm fine. It's okay. But I'm not doing this on my desk at work. I can't do that."

He licks his lips, takes a deep breath, and nods. "Okay, yeah. Okay. Give me your phone."

Wordlessly, I unlock my cell and pass it over. Vaughn taps the screen, then passes it back to me.

"I just texted myself with my address. Be there in an hour."

He kisses me once more, just as hot and needy, and then…he's gone.

I stare down at the address. It's not downtown. He's not staying at a hotel? Most actors are based out of Los Angeles and just come up here for appointments.

I'm *not* going to have sex with Vaughn Barrymore. No way.

Absolutely not.

CHAPTER 2

~OLIVIA~

"*A*bsolutely *not*," I repeat, out loud this time, and turn where the GPS tells me. "I'll just show up and politely decline. I mean, sure, it's flattering that Vaughn Barrymore is attracted to me, but that doesn't mean I'm at his beck and call for sex. That's just silly. Surely, he'll understand that and be reasonable."

I nod, satisfied with the idea. Of course, I could just text him or call since I now have his private number, but for reasons I can't explain, even to myself, I think it's more polite to do this in person.

Which is dumb because I left work early, and I'm just following orders as if he's some kind of dominant and is the boss of me.

Which he, absolutely, is *not*.

But my lips still tingle from that kiss, and I can't stop thinking about how good he smelled or how he knew exactly how to grip my hair. Not too hard to pull, but firmly enough to let me know that he meant business.

"Shit," I whisper and turn into a neighborhood I've never seen before. I drive up a hill and then onto a driveway that leads even farther to a ridiculously big house.

After I park and get out of my little Lexus, I turn and take in a long, deep breath.

Vaughn has a view of the city *and* Puget Sound. It's absolutely beautiful, and I bet the sunsets are stunning up here.

I tear myself away from the view and walk up to the tall, double front door. It's arched, like something you'd expect to see in a castle.

Before I can knock, Vaughn opens the door and lifts his lips in a half smile.

God, he's cocky.

"Hi," he says.

"Hello." I clear my throat and push my hair over my shoulder. "I came to let you know that, while I'm flattered, I'm not here to have sex with you."

He raises an eyebrow. "You came all this way just to tell me that?"

"Yes." I cross my arms over my chest and feel more than self-conscious. I really should have just texted him. "Are you renting this house?"

"No."

I tip my head to the side and want to ask so many

questions, but then I decide it's none of my business. I turn to leave.

"Okay, well, I'll see you around."

"Where are you going?"

I frown back at him, and my vagina clenches at the sight of his arm muscles in that tight, black T-shirt. Damn him. "Back to work. I have a job."

"It's past lunchtime. Why go back? You're here, aren't you? Come inside. I'll show you around." He tucks his hands behind his back. "And I won't touch you. I'd pinky promise, but I'm keeping my hands to myself."

Well, that's too bad.

I press my lips together, then shrug a shoulder and return to the doorway. "Okay. But if I stay, I get to ask some questions."

"Ask away," he says easily. He doesn't move out of my way as I brush past him to go inside, and he smells as delicious as he did just an hour ago.

This is a bad, bad idea. I should go. But, damn it, I don't want to.

I don't particularly like Vaughn, yet I can't seem to talk myself into leaving, either. It's like he's a magnet— a sexy, cocky, irritating magnet.

I might need some professional help.

"How long have you lived here?" I ask, trying to fill the silence.

"My family has owned the house for a long time. Since before I was born."

I frown over at him. "I assumed that your family was based out of LA since they're so entrenched in show business."

He shrugs and pads barefoot through a huge foyer to an open living space. "We spent most of our time in California, but they have property in a lot of places. They always liked Seattle, so we spent quite a bit of time here. I have a lot of meetings to prepare for the film, so I'm living here for the time being."

I nod and walk to the wall of windows to take in the view. "How convenient."

I suspect that if my father had raised us mostly in LA, Vaughn and I would have had a similar childhood. We both come from famous parents, but Vaughn's went much deeper than that. His grandparents, and even *their* parents, were Hollywood royalty. My dad's family was just regular people from Seattle.

When I turn to ask a question, I bump right into Vaughn's firm chest and jump.

"Sorry," he says and steadies me by resting his hands on my shoulders. "Didn't mean to startle you."

"That's what happens when you sneak up on someone."

His lips turn up into that half smile once more. It's just...dreamy. I wish he'd do it more often. "Didn't sneak."

He whispers the words, and then his right hand drifts up to gently brush my cheek, moving down my jaw. He lifts my chin so he can look into my eyes.

"Green," he says.

"Yes, your eyes are green."

He smirks. "*Your* eyes are green."

I don't say anything in return, just watch as those green orbs of his travel over my face as if he's committing every inch of it to memory.

"And you're touching me," I whisper, remembering that he'd said he would keep his hands to himself.

"You're fucking irresistible." He takes a long, deep breath. Just when I think he's about to kiss me, when he leans in as if pulled by the same magnetic force that I feel, too, and his eyes drop to my lips, he pulls away. "But you're right. I'm not touching you."

"This is silly." I shake my head and push my hands through my hair as I chuckle. "I'll just…go."

"Stay," he suggests. "You came all this way. Why did you, by the way?"

"Why did I what? Come up here?"

He nods slowly.

"I just… Well, I think—I don't know."

"Did you hate it when I kissed you?"

"No." The answer is immediate and out of my mouth before I can zip my lips shut. "No, I didn't hate it. Obviously. Because here I am."

"I didn't hate it, either."

Those green eyes of his flash, and something in me feels good because I pleased him.

What in the hell is wrong with me?

I walk to the kitchen to an island the size of Jamaica

and drag my fingertip over the cool marble. The room is *gorgeous.*

"I was so frustrated," he continues as he slowly follows me as if giving me an opportunity to run.

But my feet are firmly planted. I'm not going anywhere.

"I thought you were being completely unprofessional and wasting my time." He sweeps a piece of my hair off my cheek. "And then you just stood up for yourself and put me in my place. I've never been so turned on in my life."

He swipes his thumb across my lower lip.

"Not used to that, huh? Being put in your place?"

"No." He brushes his nose against mine. "I'm not."

"I'm not a doormat," I inform him, but my voice isn't as strong as I'd like it to be because I'm suddenly finding it hard to catch my breath. "And I wasn't the one in the wrong."

"I wrote down the wrong day," he admits. "Sorry about that."

"Are you always a jerk?"

"Sometimes."

"Well, cut it out."

That hand of his fists my hair again, the way it did earlier, and it's a direct line to my nipples, which have puckered as if they wouldn't mind if he decided to pay them some attention.

Bad nipples.

"I want to fuck you, Olivia. Right here, right now."

I swallow and watch his lips. Shit, I want him, too. Don't I? Why else would I be here? Of *course,* I want him to get me naked and do sexy things to me.

"I haven't walked out the door," I remind him, and that's all the invitation he needs.

That mouth is on mine in a millisecond, initiating a hot, bruising kiss that has me gripping his arms. His hand leaves my hair long enough to whip my top over my head, and then he spins me around, makes quick work of unfastening my bra, and cups his hands to my breasts as his teeth latch onto the flesh of my shoulder.

Thank God for skirts.

That's all I can think when he pushes me forward and flips up my hem, slipping his fingers under the elastic of my simple blue panties, finding me already wet.

I gasp.

He groans.

"Jesus, you're soaked. I want hard and fast, so tell me if it's too much."

I shake my head, but he tugs on a nipple. "I mean it. Use your words."

"Just fuck me already."

Is that *me?*

I feel him grin against my skin, and then I hear a wrapper tear, and Vaughn pushes inside me.

I gasp again and widen my stance. God, it just feels so damn *good.*

He fists his hand in my hair at the base of my scalp. Just at the right place, with the right amount of pull.

"You feel damn good," he says against my ear as he sets a rhythm that has me blind with pleasure.

The marble of the countertop is cool under me, and all I can do is hold on as I push back against him, feeling the tension building within me as I head toward that ultimate climax.

"That's it," he says and drags a hand down my spine to my ass. "Give in to it, babe. Go over."

His voice is pure sex. His hands on me are everything I never knew I needed from a man. And when he pushes back in, *hard,* I come apart.

"Yes," he growls, then pushes and grinds into me as he surrenders to his own orgasm.

He kisses my shoulder, my neck.

And then he slips out of me and pads around the island to dispose of the condom.

He didn't even take my underwear off.

I don't know why, but that's damn hot.

I take a deep breath and reach for my shirt, slipping it over my head. When I glance over at Vaughn, he's grinning and passes me a bottle of water. His pants are still undone, but he's tucked himself away, and he looks pleased with himself.

"Stay," he says simply. "I'll order in dinner, and we can just hang."

Tempting. It's more tempting than I thought it would be.

But I shake my head and take a drink of the water. "I can't. I have a lot of work to catch up on now."

"I'm not sorry," he says simply.

"Me, neither." I grin at him.

"Excellent sex is nothing to be sorry about."

I tip my head and study him, then just laugh and turn away. "You really are a cocky shit, you know that?"

"Don't even try to tell me that wasn't excellent sex."

It was maybe the hottest sex I've ever had.

"It didn't suck," I reply instead and walk to the front door. "I'll be in touch when I need you to come to the office for a fitting."

"I want to see you again." He leans on the doorjamb and pulls on my hand, yanking me against him. His lips are a mere inch from mine. "Outside of the office."

"Not a great idea."

"Best idea I've ever had."

I lift an eyebrow. "I don't think seeing each other is going to work. I know you're not used to hearing *no*. But you might just have to learn to deal with it."

"It's okay, I'll talk you into it." He kisses me once more, long and slow, and then I pull away before I say *screw it* and stay for the evening.

I wave, get in my car, and drive away.

In the rearview mirror, I see Vaughn standing in the doorway, watching me.

What in the *hell* just happened? I had sex—hot kitchen sex—with Vaughn Barrymore. What was I thinking? Have I lost my damn mind? Did I fall and hit my head, and now I've had a complete personality switch?

Instead of going back to the office, I head toward home. I want a shower and some food, and I can work on some things from my home office if I really want to.

I'm surprised to see that Stella's Range Rover is in the driveway when I pull in.

I walk inside and find her in the living room, her laptop in front of her, glasses perched on her gorgeous nose.

"You're home early," she says.

"So are you."

"I had a client in the neighborhood and decided to come here to work rather than driving back downtown."

She pulls her glasses off and narrows her eyes at me. "Who did you have sex with?"

"What?" I scoff as if she's completely off base. "I just came home early, that's all."

"Nope. You have that look you get when you've gotten laid. I know you better than *anyone*, and I know the signs. Spill it."

I shake my head, and she stands, setting her hands on her hips. "Olivia Williams, spill the tea."

"I can't tell you." I bite my lip, struggling. Stella is my *best friend.* She knows everything about everything.

But this? This could be *very* bad.

"We're the only ones here," she says. "I'm quite sure

CHAPTER 3

~VAUGHN~

"Up!" Pudgy hands lift toward me, and a little face with the sweetest lips I've ever seen pouts, wanting my attention.

"You're cute," I reply as I lift Paisley into my arms and blow a raspberry on her round cheek. "But you already know that, don't you?"

"Just like most women in the free world, our daughter has a crush on you," Kelly says as she walks into the dining room and sets out a platter of ribs. "And she's a year old."

"She has good taste," I reply and wink at Paisley, my little goddaughter. Kelly's married to my best friend, Jamal, and I've known them both for more years than I can count. I trust them implicitly.

So much so that Kelly is my personal assistant.

"I can't believe you got the appointment with costuming wrong for this project," Kelly says as Jamal walks into the room with corn on the cob and pota-toes. Jamal takes the baby from me and sets her in her high chair. It's still jarring to see my enormous friend, with his broad shoulders and huge hands, handling that tiny baby girl. "I reminded you *three times* of when to be there."

"I wrote it down wrong," I reply with a sigh. "I messed up the date. Do you know Olivia Conner?" I ask her.

"Doesn't ring a bell," she replies. "Wait. Of course, it does. She's the one you had the appointment with. I don't know her, though. I hear she's new at Williams Productions. Did you hate her? Because from the look on your face, you don't like her."

"What's the look on my face?"

"Surly," she says, tilting her head to the side as she thinks about it. Her black, curly hair bounces with the motion, and she covers her mouth with her hand as she chews. "And a little pinched. Don't do that, it's not a good look."

"I don't hate her," I reply and reach for a rib, taking a bite.

"No, he definitely doesn't hate her," Jamal says, shaking his head. "You dog. He already hit that."

"What?" Kelly demands and stares back and forth between us. "How do you know? How does *he* know?"

I just stare at my best friend as he bites into a rib and shakes his head at me.

"What the fuck?"

"Hey, man, the baby." Jamal winces and drops the clean rib bone onto his plate. "She's picking up more words now, so we don't swear around her."

"*You* don't swear?" I grin. "My friend, the famous football player, who I know better than anyone in the world, doesn't swear? Yeah, good luck with that."

Jamal's played ball in Seattle for three years, so he and Kelly settled up here. I love spending time in the Pacific Northwest, so I'm in Seattle whenever I can swing it. And Kelly can do most of her work for me remotely anyway. She can badger me just as easily over the phone as she does in person.

"Don't be an ass," Jamal says. "I mean, a jerk."

I snort, and Kelly narrows her eyes on her husband before turning back to me. "Stop changing the subject. Did you or didn't you sleep with her?"

"There was no sleeping involved."

"Vaughn Barrymore," she says sternly.

"Now you sound like my nanny." I sigh and shrug a shoulder. "I fu—hit that."

"Dude, you just can't keep it in your pants," Jamal says.

"I *can* keep it in my pants," I say dryly. "You can't just sleep around in this business. It becomes *everyone's* business. I don't know what it was about her."

Okay, that's a fucking lie. I know *exactly* what it was.

Long, thick hair that felt like silk in my hands.

Big, green eyes that I could get fucking lost in.

A body that *begs* for my hands, and tits unlike any I've ever seen before.

Jesus, just thinking about her gets me hard.

"But she's a pain in the ass," I continue. "She's got a sassy mouth on her. And she's a little...bitchy."

"Seriously?" Jamal asks and looks meaningfully at the baby.

"It's the only word I had, man."

"So, it was just one and done?" Kelly demands and adds a spoonful of mashed potatoes to the baby's tray. "Won't that be awkward when you have to go in for fittings and stuff?"

Shit, I hadn't thought about that.

And I hate the idea of being done with her.

Even if she does make me want to spank her ass because of her attitude.

"I'm going to need you to make sure my schedule's clear every evening for the next two weeks," I inform Kelly, who raises a perfect eyebrow.

"Why?"

"Because, apparently, I'm a masochist," I reply. "I don't think there's much going on anyway."

"Only dinners and parties and appearances," she says and looks as if she wants to quit on me. "I can get you out of most of it, but you can't miss the dinner in LA next week. You're speaking, and we committed to it six months ago."

"Okay, just cancel the rest then."

"Done."

"You're gonna keep hitting that, aren't you?" Jamal says with a wide smile. "You like the sassy girl."

"Yeah, I'm gonna see her some more. And decide if I like her."

"Maybe she doesn't like *you*, and I'll be canceling all of these plans for nothing."

"If that's the case, I'll enjoy some quiet time, won't I?"

"If that's the case," Kelly says while shaking her head, "you'll let me know so I can reschedule some of it. You have a movie to promote, a documentary about your family to comment on, and a whole host of things that you already know about. You don't get to just go on vacation for the next two weeks, Vaughn."

"You're not the boss of me."

Jamal tosses his head back and laughs like a damn loon. "Yeah, she is. She's the boss of all of us."

"That's right," Kelly says with satisfaction. "I am. And it's a good thing, too, because you two would be lost without me."

"How do you manage it?" I ask her.

"Black girl magic," she says with a toss of her bouncy curls.

I open my mouth, but Jamal shakes his head. "Don't argue, man. Just don't."

THE GAME IS ON. I'm a big Lakers fan and usually have courtside seats when I'm in town. Tonight, I have to settle for the monster TV in the media room of the Seattle house.

It's not exactly a hardship, but it's also not the same as being there. It's not the same as having Lebron practically sweating on you as he runs by.

And when I watch the game at home, I have too much damn time to think.

I haven't been able to think about anything but Olivia since she left my house yesterday afternoon. Dinner with Jamal and Kelly was a nice distraction this evening, but now I'm alone again, and all I can think about is *her.*

Gorgeous body.

Sassy mouth.

The constant lust is almost annoying now.

Rather than sit around and be sexually frustrated, I should just call her.

So, I do.

I dial her number. After two rings, it goes to voicemail.

I scowl at the screen and see a text come through from Olivia.

Olivia: DID YOU WANT SOMETHING?

Me: YEAH, I WANT YOU TO CALL ME.

Olivia: WHY? PEOPLE DON'T CALL. THEY TEXT.

I scoff and redial her number. It rings once.

"Come on, pick up."

Rings twice.

"Pick up, or I'll spank your gorgeous little ass."

It rings three times, and then she picks up.

"Uh, hello?"

"Why are you avoiding me?"

She's quiet for a moment, and I can almost picture her narrowing her eyes at me.

Even that turns me the fuck on.

"If you behaved like a normal person and simply *texted* me, I wouldn't be avoiding you."

"Do you have issues with talking on the phone?"

"Doesn't everyone?" she counters, making me grin. "So, what's up?"

I sigh and mute the TV, watching as Lebron dunks the ball.

"I was just wondering what you're up to, that's all. And, yeah, I could have just texted, but then I wouldn't be able to hear your sexy voice, and that would be a shame."

She goes quiet again.

"Did you hang up on me?"

"No." I hear the smile in her voice and relax just a little. "I'm not up to much. I worked late and then came home, made dinner for the crew, got cozy, and was reading a book."

"Who's the crew?"

I settle back in my chair, enjoying her already. Her voice is soothing—like liquid chocolate.

"I share a house with a few of my cousins," she says.

"And we take turns cooking dinner. Except for Drew. When it's his turn, he orders pizza or something, which is fine with me because I'm pretty sure he could burn boiled water."

"Who are the other cousins?" I just want to keep her talking.

"Stella and Erin. Drew is the only boy. And, technically, he lives in the guest house, but he comes into the main house to eat our food and hang."

"Aside from my family, I've never lived with roommates," I confess.

I've never needed them.

"I like it. It's never boring."

She's quiet for a moment, and I try to picture what she looks like.

"What are you wearing?" I ask her.

"Don't be a perv, Vaughn."

I laugh and tap my screen, engaging the video chat option. After a few seconds, Olivia's gorgeous face comes on my screen.

And she's not at all what I expected.

Her hair is up in a bun, she's wearing a hoodie, and her face is clean of makeup. She's also wearing glasses.

"Not exactly glamorous," she says.

"Better," I reply and rub my fingers with my thumb. I itch to touch her. To kiss her.

"I did say that I got cozy."

"Did I imply that I think you're *not* hot right now?"

She raises a brow and then shrugs a shoulder. "No. I suppose not. What is that you're wearing?"

"Lucky T-shirt." I hold the phone away so she can see my shirt. "I always wear it when the Lakers play."

"Lakers fan, huh?" she says with a grin.

"To the bone," I agree. "I'm usually there in person when I can swing it."

"Instead, you're in Seattle and talking to me."

"It's not a bad trade." She grins, and I have to take a deep breath. Jesus, she just gets right under my skin. "You might be the most beautiful woman I've ever seen in my life."

That grin fades, and she looks somewhere over the phone.

"Why does that make you uncomfortable?"

"It doesn't."

"Don't lie to me," I whisper. "It's no secret that I'm incredibly attracted to you, Olivia."

"Liv," she says. "You can call me Liv."

I'll call her Olivia. I like it.

"If I make you uncomfortable, just say so. No hard feelings."

She blows out a breath and shakes her head. "It's not that. And I won't pretend that I'm not attracted to you, too. Because, clearly, I am. You haven't made me uncomfortable or done anything that I didn't want you to do."

"I'm really not creepy."

She laughs, and my stomach loosens. My dick, however, tightens.

"Creepy dudes don't know that they're creepy."

I smile at her. "True. So, here's more truth for you. You turn me the hell on."

Those green eyes shine with interest. "Yeah?"

"Yeah."

"Well, that's not necessarily a bad thing."

"It is when you're not here."

She bites her plump lower lip. God, does she know that she's being fucking coy? I want to bite that lip.

"You do?"

"Did I say that out loud?"

"Yeah."

I nod slowly. "Yeah, I do."

She clears her throat and squirms in her seat.

"Do I turn you on, too?"

"I mean, have you met you? You're walking sex on a stick. I haven't seen the dimples above your ass in person yet, but...yeah, you're pretty sexy, Vaughn."

She quickly covers her mouth with her hand and stares down at the phone in horror.

"Oh, shit. I said that, didn't I?"

"I guess we're in the mood for confessions." And I like that she included the word *yet*.

That means she wants to see more of me.

Which is a damn good thing because I want to see a hell of a lot more of her.

"How do you feel when you're turned on, Liv? Do you get a little warm?"

She nods.

"What else do you feel?"

She shrugs, pressing her lips together.

"Don't be shy," I urge. "I'm hard as a rock. Just thinking about you turns me on. Do you want me to touch myself?"

She bites that lip and looks down as if she can see through the phone like a window and then nods. "Yeah, I think you should."

"I will if you do."

She shifts in her seat, and I can tell that she's taking off her pants. I unzip my jeans and set myself free, giving my dick a couple of firm tugs. When she closes her eyes and sighs with pleasure, I have to grit my teeth to keep myself from coming right on the spot.

"What does it feel like?" I ask her.

"Wet," she says, her breath coming faster now. "A little swollen, but in a good way, you know?"

"Yeah," I say with a smile as I jerk myself. "I know. What else?"

"The base of my spine tingles." She licks her lips, and frown lines form between her eyebrows. "Ah, shit."

"That's it, babe. Shit, I wish I could be there. Now, stop. Do you hear me? Stop touching yourself, Olivia."

Her eyes spring open, and she scowls at me. "What? Why?"

"Because I said so." God, I want to kiss her. "Take a

deep breath. If I were there, my face would be between your legs. I want to taste you and drive you insane with my tongue."

"You're gonna make me touch myself again, Vaughn."

"Do it." Her arm moves again, and she sighs out a breath. "Imagine that it's me down there, my tongue on your clit, my fingers inside you. I push your legs wide and fucking devour you, Olivia."

"God, yes."

"Next time, I won't go fast with you. I'm going to take my time and explore every fucking inch of you. I'm going to make you wild and then do it all over again. I'm going to ruin you for all other men, Olivia."

"Fuck," she whispers, and I know she's close. Hell, *I'm* close.

"Go over," I coax her. "Do it."

She arches, her head falling back as her mouth opens in a silent moan, and that's all I can take. I come hard and long and make a monumental mess.

And I don't give a shit.

"Whew," Olivia says and grins at me. "That was unexpected and fun. You okay over there?"

"Come over, and I'll show you how good I am."

She laughs, and I grin at her.

"I don't think you're kidding."

"I'm not."

"I have an early workday tomorrow," she says with a sigh. "So, I'd better stay home tonight."

"What are you doing tomorrow night?"

"I'm hanging out with you."

No pretense. No games. It's a breath of fresh air.

"Hell, yes, you are. Just come here when you're done with work. I'll feed you and everything."

"What, exactly, are you going to feed me?"

"Are you allergic to anything?"

"No."

"Anything that makes you sick to your stomach because you find it gross?"

"Uh, anchovies. Snails. Let's stay away from anything slimy."

"No oysters, then."

She wrinkles her nose and shakes her head. "No. No, thanks."

"I got you covered," I promise her.

"I'll text you when I'm on my way. I usually leave the office by about six."

"That works. Have a good day tomorrow, okay?"

"Okay. Goodnight, Vaughn."

"'Night."

I hang up and stare at the silent TV as the announcers talk about the game that's now finished.

I don't even know who won.

And I don't care.

After knowing her for about forty-eight hours, Olivia has me all tied up in knots. I don't remember the last time this happened. Have I ever had such a crush on a woman? Besides that time I worked with Sandra

Bullock and swore to anyone who would listen that I was going to marry her.

Sandy's still a friend.

But I was nineteen, and I don't think that counts.

Besides, I'm not *marrying* Olivia.

I'm just going to enjoy her for as long as we're both inclined to do so. Then, I'll walk away, no harm to anyone involved.

Simple.

But something tells me that this won't be simple at all. I should go back to LA and get on with my life. Because once I get involved with Olivia, I don't think I'll want to walk away.

I don't have room in my life for a serious relationship.

But I know that I can't leave now. I need more of Olivia like I need air to breathe.

So, no, I'm not going anywhere until I've had my fill of this woman.

Tomorrow can't get here fast enough.

CHAPTER 4

~OLIVIA~

"*O*kay, hold your arms out like this." I hold mine perpendicular to my body, and Adam Carter, one of the stars of the movie I'm working on, follows suit. He's handsome as sin and always plays the bad guy.

Which, if I'm being honest, I kind of love.

Why are women always so attracted to the bad boys? I'll have to bring that up with Stella over a glass of wine so we can figure it out.

"I was excited to work with you," Adam says kindly. He may play a villain, but he's one of the nicest actors I've ever had in my office.

Unlike a certain someone whose name rhymes with *gone.*

"Why is that?" I ask and jot down the measurements. Adam has a killer chest. In fact, he's muscly in all the right places.

"I loved the work you did on *Small Town Girl*," he says, and I raise an eyebrow.

"You pay attention to the costume designers that work on movies?"

"Of course, I do. This is my job. I pay attention to everything, and you're good at what you do."

I feel my cheeks flush and smile gratefully. "Thanks. I enjoy it a lot."

I turn Adam away from me and measure his shoulders and arms, wrists, and then his neck.

"The costumes for this movie are quite elaborate," I continue.

"Period pieces usually are. You have your work cut out for you. It's a big cast."

"With a few hundred extras, thanks to war scenes," I agree with a smile. "But we'll get it done. I have an excellent, talented staff."

"I'm sure you'll do great and make it look effortless."

He looks as if he wants to say something, but before he can, I blurt out, "Why do you always play the bad guy?"

His eyebrows wing up.

"I mean, I've seen your movies." I just keep going as if my lips can't stop moving. Why does this guy make me so nervous? "And you're always the villain. Why is that? Are you being typecast?"

I move away and put my tape measure on the desk, then continue to jot some notes.

"I like it, actually," Adam replies, and I glance over at

him. He's well over six feet tall with blond hair and the most striking blue eyes. The camera eats him up. "The characters are so different from me, and it's fun to be a little bad sometimes. Bonus when I'm being *paid* to be a jerk."

I laugh and then shrug. "I guess I can see that. Good point. What's your shoe size?"

"Twelve," he says. "What's your phone number?"

I open my mouth and then stop, turning back to him once more. "Pardon?"

"Your phone number," he repeats and holds my gaze with confidence.

"Oh, um, I don't think—"

"It's okay," he says smoothly. "Point taken. When will you need me back for the next fitting?"

"In a couple of weeks," I reply and feel awkward. What's the harm in giving him my number? "My assistant will make the arrangements with yours."

"I look forward to seeing you in a couple of weeks, then," Adam says just as Vaughn comes walking through my open door, eyes narrowing on me.

"I didn't mean to interrupt."

"Not at all," Adam says. "We were just finishing up here."

He nods at me, pats Vaughn on the shoulder, and leaves the office, closing the door behind him.

"What are you doing here?" I ask, feeling flustered. *Flushed.*

Vaughn must notice because he just slowly walks to

me and cups my face in his hand. *And there go the damn butterflies.* He stares down at me as if he's searching for something.

"I thought I'd surprise you. Did you give him your number?"

"What? No. Wait, it's not your business if I did."

He raises just one eyebrow at that. "It's not?"

"No."

"Hmm." He leans closer as he drags his thumb across my bottom lip. I stick my tongue out, just barely touching his skin. He sucks in a breath. "I think it is. Because all I can think about is you, and if someone else is in the picture, I'd like to know."

I clear my throat. Before I can say anything, he presses his lips to mine. This kiss isn't wild and frenzied; it's soft and sweet. Still hot as hell, but he's not in a hurry. His lips are silky and sure, and my hands fist in his shirt at his sides as I hold on and give in to the kiss. He smells like sin and bad choices, and I don't even care.

I press against him, and the sexiest groan ever slips out of his throat.

"Jesus, you're sweet," he whispers, then boosts me onto my desk and spreads my legs. "Why can't I get enough of you?"

I can't answer him. I just sigh when his hand journeys up my bare thigh, under the hem of my brown skirt. When his fingertips brush over my panties, I gasp.

"So responsive," he whispers. "So damn *good.*"

I lean my forehead on his shoulder when his finger slips under the elastic and finds me wet and needy.

Just two light brushes over my clit, and I'm trembling. One more, and I'm ready to come apart, right here on my damn desk.

"Don't come," he mutters, then pulls away and licks his finger.

"What are you doing?" Blood rushes back to my head, and I see red when Vaughn simply grins in that cocky way he does. "Get back here and finish that."

"I'll finish it later," he says. "I'll see you at six. As we planned."

"So, you came all the way downtown just to frustrate me?"

"No, I just wanted to see you. *That* was a bonus."

He gives me an arrogant wink, and then he's out my door, leaving me a throbbing, needy woman who just let a man *tease* her.

In my own office!

"Oh, hell no," I mutter, shaking my head as I jump off my desk and straighten my skirt. "I certainly will *not* be going over there this evening."

"Honey, I'm home!" Drew calls out from the back door.

"In the living room," I call back as he comes in, a

Vitamin Water in his hand. He sits in the chair across from me. "How was your day?"

"Good." He sips. "Lots of meetings."

"Well, you're an important football coach. Of course, you have a lot of meetings."

"I'm an offensive line coach for a university," he reminds me with a shrug. "Not too fancy there. But I like it. Hell, I'm just happy to still be a part of the game."

Drew played college ball and was good, but not professional-good like our uncle Will. Still, he always knew that he wanted to be involved in the sport, so taking on a coaching job was ideal for him. Someday, he hopes to fulfill his dream of being a professional head coach.

He'll get there.

"How about you?" he counters. "How was your day?"

"Meh. It was a day. Not too bad, I guess."

Not until Vaughn showed up and tried to kill me with sexual frustration.

The jerk.

"Do you have plans tonight?" Drew asks. "I think I'm going over to my parents' house. Dad has a project he needs some help with. Lawnmower or something he's fixing."

"My plans fell through, so I think I'll just be hanging out here."

My phone starts to ring, and I stare down at it,

seeing Vaughn's name on the readout. I check the time, and it's 6:01 p.m.

I dismiss the call and turn to Drew.

"Probably just someone trying to sell me a vehicle warranty."

"They just don't give up," he agrees as my phone pings with a text.

Vaughn: WHERE ARE YOU? CALL ME.

"I'm gonna head out," Drew says. "I'll see you later, cuz."

"Tell Uncle Caleb and Aunt Brynna hi for me."

"Will do."

He walks out, and my phone rings with another call. This time, it's a number I don't recognize.

"Are you seriously calling me from another number? Can't you just take a hint?"

There's a moment of silence.

"Is this Olivia?"

That's *not* Vaughn's voice. I squeeze my eyes closed and think: *Shit.*

"Yes, this is she."

"Great. Hi, it's Adam."

I blink in surprise. "Adam? This is unexpected."

"I know, and I hope you won't hold it against me for getting your number from my assistant. Look, I won't play games here, okay? I think you're a smart, beautiful woman, and I'd love to take you out to dinner."

"Tonight?"

"If you're free," Adam confirms. "Or any night, really."

I bite my lip, considering. Before I can think any more about it, I say, "Sure. I'd love to. Tonight works for me, actually. Where should I meet you?"

He suggests a restaurant downtown that I know, and I hang up to go get ready. All I have to do is freshen my makeup and change into jeans and a green sweater.

My phone pings with another text.

Vaughn: WHAT THE HELL, LIV?

Sure, the adult thing to do would be to text him back, but I'm completely annoyed with him and would probably say something snide. I'd rather just ignore him. In fact, I turn the phone off altogether and drop it into my purse.

I'd leave it at home, but that's not smart. I should have it with me in case of an emergency.

The drive back into the city isn't too bad, and when I approach the door of the restaurant, I see Adam standing on the sidewalk, waiting for me.

"Hey," I say and see his face transform into a wide smile when he sees me. Adam takes my hand and leans in to kiss my cheek.

"You're a vision," he says. "Thanks for meeting me."

"Thanks for the invitation."

"I hope you're hungry."

"I'm *starving*. And I love Mexican food, so this is perfect."

"Excellent."

Adam leads me inside, and the hostess escorts us to a table in the corner. I'm surprised that no one pays much attention to him as we pass by the tables.

"So, you got my number from your assistant?" I ask once we're seated.

"I did," he replies without any attempt at a lie or a coverup.

I respect that.

"And if you'd told me to fuck off, I would have," he assures me.

"I probably wouldn't have said it like that." I sip my ice water, contemplating. "I might have said: *'No means no.'*"

"Ouch." Adam winces. "Fair point. But there's no harm in trying, right?"

"That's true. How long are you in Seattle?"

"Just until tomorrow," he says. "I arrived yesterday for meetings and your fitting today. I go back to LA in the morning."

"Quick trip."

"Story of my life," he says with a shrug. "I'm never in one place for long. I bounce from movie sets all over the place to LA, to wherever else I'm needed, really. I don't know why I bought a house. I'm never there."

"Real estate is never a bad investment."

His eyes narrow on me as he pops a chip and salsa into his mouth, and then he grins. "I suppose you're right. And I'm not complaining. I like my job."

"I get it. I like having my home base. I'm a homebody when I'm not in the office."

"Do you spend much time in LA?"

"Never been," I reply honestly. My father is down there often, but I've never gone. It wasn't allowed when I was a kid, and I haven't had time as an adult. "It's never been on my list of must-see places."

"Well, if you want to come down, I can show you around anytime. You know, we can see the usual places. Spago. The Hollywood sign. Pink's hotdog stand."

"I sense a food theme here."

"I'm a food fan," he says with a grin. "Do you like sports?"

"Sure. Shopping is my favorite sport."

Adam sits back as the waitress delivers his burrito, along with my carne asada, and his eyes laugh at me as the server makes sure we have everything we need. Once she's gone, he tilts his head to the side. "Shopping is a sport?"

"Oh, hell yes. The way I do it, it is."

I am my mother's daughter, after all.

"Aside from that? Not really. You?"

"Yeah, I am. Maybe it's a guy thing."

"Maybe it's a human thing. I have girls in my life who *love* sports. I do like football."

"Do you have a favorite team?"

"Seattle, of course."

"Right. You live here. Makes sense."

"When your uncle is the most famous Seattle player ever, you kind of learn to love the game."

"Who's your uncle?"

Shit. I didn't mean to let that slip. "Oh, it's no big deal."

Adam sits back and stares at me. "Maybe it is. Who's your uncle?"

"Will Montgomery," I say and sip my water.

Adam's eyebrows climb into his hairline. "Wait. What? That means you're...Luke's daughter?"

"There are a *lot* of people in the family," I begin, but then sigh in defeat. "Yeah. I'm Luke's daughter."

"But you said your last name was Conner when I arrived earlier today."

"Yeah. I took my mother's maiden name professionally. It's just...easier. Less judgy. Less pressure."

"And you've never been to LA?"

"No. My dad had interesting rules when we were small. Mostly, he tried to protect us."

"He's very private from what I understand," Adam agrees. "I don't know him well, but he's incredibly well respected. I admire him very much."

"I do, too."

I like Adam. I don't feel any kind of romantic spark here, but I enjoy his company a lot.

Dinner flies by, and before I know it, we're back on the sidewalk.

"Thanks for dinner," I say as he takes my hand once more. "I had a good time. It was nice to meet you."

"Same here." His smile is kind as he leans over and kisses my forehead. "I'd ask you out again, but I get the feeling that you'd turn me down."

I sigh and cringe. "If I'm being honest, you're probably right. But it's not because you're not charming and handsome and kind."

"No spark," he says with a nod. "I get it. But I do like you, even if we're just friends."

"Hey, there's no *just* there. Finding friends, especially in this business, isn't easy."

"Yeah, I do like you." He nods once more. "Fair point. Drive home safely, and I'll see you in a couple of weeks. I hope we can stay in touch, even as friends."

"Sounds good to me. Safe travels tomorrow."

He sets off down the sidewalk, and I turn toward my car, parked in the opposite direction.

It's kind of a bummer that there's no sexual attraction there. Adam is kind, considerate, smart...all the good things. But he's not the one for me.

And I wasn't kidding about the friend thing. It's not easy to make true friends when it comes to show business.

I think Adam and I will be good friends.

Satisfied with that, I drive back home, not surprised to see that no one else is there when I arrive.

I make my way upstairs, wash my face, and change into comfortable sweats and a T-shirt that says: MONDAYS CAN SUCK IT. Just as I sit in the chair in the corner of my bedroom where I can sit and watch Puget

Sound in the distance, Stella walks into the room with two glasses of wine and concern in her gorgeous blue eyes.

"Hey. I didn't know you were home."

"Just got here about fifteen minutes ago," she says, passing me a glass.

"What's the occasion?"

"Have you been online at all?"

"Uh, no. I turned off my phone. Why?"

Without another word, Stella sets her glass aside and opens her phone. After a few taps on the screen, she hands it to me.

"Just look."

Vaughn. He's grinning and has his arm slung around the waist of a gorgeous woman with a mane of curly, black hair. She's looking at him with adoration.

"Okay."

"It was taken *tonight*."

My stomach jitters. Tonight? So, when I didn't show up, he found the first willing tart to go out with?

"It's a free world," I reply and pass the phone back to her.

"Yeah, but you said you were having dinner with him tonight."

"I canceled."

Stella drinks her wine. "Why?"

I stand and close my door in case one of the other roomies comes home. Then, I return to my chair and my wine.

"Because he showed up at my office today and totally frustrated me. Sexually. Like, he moved in all sexy-like but wouldn't let me come and then said he'd finish things *later*."

"Ew." She scrunches up her nose. "Why do guys think that's hot? It's not hot at all."

"Right? Exactly! It pissed me off, so I didn't go over for dinner."

"And now he's being a child about it," she finishes for me.

"That's the way I see it. I did go out for dinner, though. Adam Carter asked me to go, and I went."

"Adam Carter, the *actor*?"

"Yeah. It was literally *just* dinner, Stel. He's really nice, but there's no spark there. I guess I made a new friend today."

"Well, aren't you the popular one?"

"It's weird." I shrug.

"It's not weird at all. You're a hot, successful woman. Why wouldn't celebrities trip over themselves to be with you?"

"You're good for my ego."

She smirks and pulls chocolate out of her pocket. "Wanna share?"

"I'm not dead, Stella. Of course, I want to share."

She breaks the bar in half and passes me a piece.

"Are you going to turn your phone back on?"

"Tomorrow. If my parents need to reach me, they'll call you when they can't get through on my phone."

"Fair enough."

"Here's a question for you. I was thinking about this earlier today while taking Adam's measurements—that's how we met."

"I'm in the wrong business. Okay, shoot."

"Why do women always like the bad guys? Like, Adam always plays the villain in movies, and I think he's *so* handsome. In real life, he's a sweetheart."

"Is that why you only want to be friends? Because he's a sweetheart?"

"No." I frown and chew on the last bite of candy. "No, that can't be why."

"Vaughn's the *bad boy* in this scenario, and he's the one you're sexually attracted to. It's an interesting situation."

"There's no *situation*. I'm not seeing him again. I don't play stupid games like that. I mean, yeah, he's ridiculously sexy, but what he did today was a dick move."

"Or a lack of one," she says with a wink, and we dissolve into giggles.

"You're so clever. The point is, that's not sexy. He lost all his sexy points in my office today. And Adam's nice, but there's no chemistry. So, I'll just go back to my boring life."

"You get to put your hands all over sexy movie stars, honey. Your life is *anything* but boring."

I laugh and gulp the last of my wine. "It really is a

killer job, right? I mean, I was all up in Adam's business today. The man is *hung.*"

"Oh, my God! How do you know that?"

"Because I have to measure the inseam. Here, I'll show you. Stand up."

She does as I say, and I nudge her legs apart and crouch before her.

"So, I start with the tape measure in the crotch."

"Holy shit."

"And pull it down the leg to the top of the foot. So my hand is all up in their business."

"Ahem."

Without moving away, both of our heads turn to the doorway where Drew and Erin are standing, watching. I didn't even hear them open the door.

"If you weren't related to me, this might be hot," Drew says.

Erin snorts.

"I'm showing her how I measure an inseam."

"Sure. We'll go with that." Drew winks. "We're watching some lame-ass chick flick downstairs. Come down with us."

"It's not lame," Erin says as she follows him down the hallway to the stairs. "It's my turn to pick, and I'm not going to watch things getting blown up for two hours."

"I'm up for a girl movie," I say as I stand.

"I'm really pissed that you never told me this little

secret before, so I, too, could go into your line of work and feel up hot dudes all day."

"There are some things I have to keep for myself."

"You're a better friend than that, Liv."

I laugh and take her hand as we walk down to join the others for the movie.

"I'll make you extra popcorn, just the way you like it, to make it up to you."

"Fine." She sighs deeply, then laughs. "I wonder if we have any M&Ms."

"I think we can scrounge some up."

CHAPTER 5

~VAUGHN~

"*I*'m so glad you called and suggested we come out for a while," Kelly says with a wide smile. She and Jamal just came off the dance floor. "We haven't done something like this in a long time."

"The nanny wasn't impressed," Jamal says and sips his water. Jamal hasn't had a drop of alcohol since college. He's too in tune with his athletic job to take on the calories and side effects of alcohol.

But he loves to dance.

"She didn't mind," Kelly says with a shrug. "The baby's just sleeping anyway. So, Vaughn, how are you?"

"Me?" I shrug my shoulders. "I'm fine."

Not exactly *fine*. I'm pissed and frustrated and generally in a bad mood, but that's not Kelly's fault.

"Are you bored yet?"

"Me?" I ask again. "I'm not bored. Why do you think I'm bored?"

Kelly exchanges a look with her husband. "Because you're in Seattle, you're alone most of the time, and I know you very well. Maybe better than you know yourself. You don't enjoy being alone."

"That's ridiculous."

"No, she's right," Jamal says and reaches for the nachos in the middle of the table. "You hate being alone."

"You're both wrong." I sigh and then look at Kelly. "Did you already cancel all of my engagements over the next few weeks?"

"I was going to send the email tomorrow."

"Yeah, well, don't. It's fine. I'm available."

Jamal stops chewing. "Why?"

"It didn't work out with the costume designer." I shrug again as if it's no big deal.

Jamal and Kelly stare at each other and then bust up into hilarity. Kelly laughs so hard she has to wipe tears from her eyes.

"I'm so happy to see that you find this amusing."

"She ditched you," Kelly says.

"You don't know that. Maybe I ended it with *her*."

"Nah, if that were the case, you would have led with that," Jamal says. "What reason did she give you? I gotta know."

"Why?"

"Because I do believe that in the entire twenty-some years that I've known you, this is the first time you've ever been dumped."

"Did she give you the whole it's-not-you-it's-me line?" Kelly asks.

"No." I take a pull on my beer. "She ghosted me."

They're both stunned silent, and then they start laughing again.

"You know what? Fuck this. I'm going home."

I stand to leave, and Kelly takes my hand, pulling me back down. "No, don't go. I'm sorry, we're being complete jerks. You're right."

She takes a deep breath, trying to calm her laughter.

Jamal doesn't even try not to laugh.

My friends are assholes.

I stare at Jamal until he calms down, wipes his face, and shakes his big, bald head. "Never thought I'd see the day, bro."

"I'm fine, in case anyone's wondering."

"Wait." Kelly sits back in her seat and watches me. "She hurt your feelings. Vaughn, I'm sorry."

"No, she didn't."

She totally did, but it'll be a cold day in hell before I admit that to these two.

"What actually happened?" Kelly asks. "I need the details."

"I went to her office today just to say hi. Kissed her, told her I'd see her later, and...she never showed."

"Did you call her?" Jamal asks.

"No, I sent her a smoke signal. Of course, I called her, you idiot."

"And she didn't respond to your texts or calls?" Kelly says.

"Nope." I sip my beer. "When I called the last time, and it went straight to voicemail, I decided to stop trying. I'll be damned if I chase her."

"You have no reason to chase her," Jamal says. "A thousand girls are lined up behind her. Maybe more."

"Trust me, I see his fan mail," Kelly says. "There are plenty more. But that's not the point. I could tell that you liked her, so I'm sorry it didn't work out."

"It's just one of those things, right?"

"Yeah, one of those things that don't happen to you," Jamal responds. "It's going to be awkward when you have to work with her."

Fuck.

I hadn't even considered that. Yeah, it will be awkward as hell.

"And that's why you shouldn't try to date people you work with," Kelly reminds us all.

"I didn't *date* her," I say defensively.

"No, you just fucked her. And that's worse," she says. "It's a complete dick move. Anyway, good luck with that. Also, can you babysit tomorrow?"

I raise a brow. "That's one way to change the subject."

"There's no good segue from that," she says with a laugh. "We have an appointment, and it's the nanny's day off. It'll only be for about an hour or so."

"You know I don't mind spending time with Paisley.

71

What time?"

"Around noon?" Kelly says.

"I'll be ready for her. At least, I can hang out with one girl who likes me."

"Aw, poor Vaughn," Jamal says as he pays the tab. "He just got dumped for the first time in his life. It's a milestone, man. Like the first time you shave or when you get your driver's license. We should take a picture of you for the scrapbook."

"Suck it," I suggest, making him laugh. "How an ugly jerk like you produced the most perfect baby in the world is beyond me."

"The baby is all her mother," Jamal says. "And thank Jesus for it."

"You're not kidding."

KELLY AND JAMAL should be here with the baby anytime. I have Paisley's play area set up in the casual family room, and I have her favorite snacks.

I'm ready.

Now, I'm just pacing the house while waiting for them. Kelly wasn't off the mark last night when she'd asked me if I was bored.

I'm out of my freaking mind with boredom. I love Seattle, but I don't have a community here like I do in LA. But my best friends are here, and LA isn't exactly good for me.

The circle of people that I know there contains a lot of toxic people.

And, to be honest, I get bored of them, too.

I don't know why I'm not content in my life. And that's a lame comment because I have an awesome one.

The kind that people dream of.

I check my phone for the twentieth time and then decide *fuck it* and open a text to Olivia.

Me: HEY. I REALIZE I DID OR SAID SOMETHING TO PISS YOU OFF. THAT WASN'T MY INTENTION. WOULD YOU PLEASE JUST LET ME KNOW THAT YOU'RE OKAY? I JUST WANT TO KNOW THAT YOU'RE SAFE. THANKS.

I hit send just as the doorbell rings.

"Hey, Uncle Vaughn," Kelly says and kisses her daughter on the cheek. "We're here to destroy your pretty house."

"How dare you imply that my perfect goddaughter would destroy anything?" I reply as I take the little girl from Kelly and whisper in her ear, "You're a perfect angel, right?"

"Bon!" she announces, and I stare at Kelly in shock.

"She said my name!"

"We've been practicing," Kelly says as we wait for Jamal to bring the baby bag in from the car. "I thought you'd get a kick out of that."

"You're a genius," I inform the little girl. "Absolutely brilliant."

"Bon," she repeats happily.

"I don't know why we have to drag all of this sh—

73

stuff all the way over here for just an hour, but I do what I'm told," Jamal says as he sets the bag on my dining table. "You'll never need all of this."

"I just changed her," Kelly informs me. "And she had lunch about thirty minutes ago, so she's fed and happy. But there are snacks in there, just in case."

"I bought snacks," I inform them.

"What kind?" Kelly wants to know and marches into the kitchen.

"Oh, you know...chips and beer. Popcorn. All of the things babies love."

"Good one." Jamal gives me a fist bump.

"Aw, how did you know what all of her favorite things are?" Kelly calls from the kitchen.

"I pay attention. It's not like it's a big baby mystery or something. Even *I* like Cheerios. We'll share. Won't we, princess?"

"Bon," she repeats and pats my cheek. "My Bon."

Well, if that doesn't melt a person's heart, I don't know what will.

"My Paisley," I reply and kiss her forehead. "You guys go on. We'll be great here. I've babysat before."

"I know, but she's getting more mobile, and I don't want her to overwhelm you," Kelly says.

"Go away," I repeat, shooing them to the door. "Tell Mommy and Daddy to go, P. Say, *'bye-bye.'*"

"Bye-bye," Paisley says and then grins at me, scrunching her adorable nose. "Bye-bye, Bon."

"No, you're staying with Bon," I say and kiss her as I

close the door behind my friends. "We're going to have some fun, right?"

She sobers when she realizes that her parents just left without her. "Mama?"

"They'll be back soon. I promise. We're just gonna hang for a little while. Do you want snacks?"

"Nack," she confirms.

Jesus, she's one. Why is she already talking? I'm not ready for this.

"Okay, let's get a snack. Then we can check out all the fun toys I bought for you. We can play and snack at the same time."

I dance her around the kitchen as I pour some Cheerios into a small bowl, then I grab her sippy cup from her bag. With both my hands and my arms full, I take her to her makeshift playroom.

"Oh!" she exclaims with joy and kicks her legs to get down. She crawls over to a play kitchen and starts to bang a pot on the little stove.

"Wanna make some soup?" I ask. Before long, Paisley and I have made a gourmet pretend meal fit for a king.

Of course, she spilled her Cheerios all over the floor and then proceeded to eat them off said floor, but it's clean.

And I won't tell her mom.

The doorbell rings, and Paisley and I look at each other.

"Mama?"

"Hmm, I don't know." I stand, scoop her up, and walk to the front door. I open it, but instead of Kelly and Jamal, it's Olivia.

A punch to the gut.

A slap in the face.

I still want her so badly I ache with it.

And that pretty much pisses me off.

She opens her mouth to speak, then stops short when she sees the baby on my hip.

"Uh, hi."

"Hey," I reply.

Olivia raises an eyebrow at me in question.

"I'm babysitting," I say but step back in invitation for Olivia to come inside. "Come on in."

"Thanks. I got your text and thought it might be easier if I just stopped by."

"Driving all the way across town to get here is easier than typing out a quick text that says, *'I'm okay?'*"

She narrows her eyes and bites her lip, and I feel like a bit of an ass.

But only a bit.

Because she's the one who ghosted *me*, not the other way around.

I lead her into the living room and sit on the couch with the baby on my lap. Paisley watches Liv as Liv sits across from us and takes a long, deep breath.

"Bon," Paisley says and pats my cheek.

"Aw, she says your name," Liv says with a smile.

"She's beautiful. I've never seen so much dark hair on a baby, and I've been around my share."

"She looks just like her mom, thank goodness." I grin and kiss the baby, then look over at the first woman who's ever made me nervous. "So, what's up?"

"Well, I wanted to tell you, *in person*, that I'm sorry I ignored you last night. I should have just texted you and told you that I wasn't going to come over here."

"Yeah, you probably should have. Why didn't you?"

"Because you made me *really* mad."

I blink at her. "What? How did I manage that?"

"That"—she waves her hand around in the air—"thing you pulled in my office."

"I kissed you."

"Oh, no. No, you didn't just *kiss* me, Vaughn."

"Bon," Paisley repeats helpfully.

"I *did* kiss you, Olivia."

"And then you teased me. And that's not cool. I don't know why guys think it's playful or sexy or whatever, but it's *not*. It's annoying. And, honestly, it's childish. You don't like"—she waves her hand again and then whispers—"blue balls."

"No, I don't."

"Well, there you have it. You were pissed because of Adam or something, and you punished me. And I will not have that."

"Okay." Paisley pats my cheek, but I ignore her. "I hear you, and I can see your point. If the situation had been reversed, it would have made me mad, too."

"Exactly."

Paisley pats my cheek again, so I kiss her palm.

"But you should have said something."

"I did. If you remember correctly, I told you to get back there and finish what you started. And you smirked at me. *Smirked* at me."

She's clearly getting heated about it again, so I calmly reply with, "Okay. Okay, I'm sorry. I truly am. I thought I was being flirty and charming."

Olivia snorts. "No. There's nothing flirty *or* charming about that shit."

"Bon," Paisley demands, still patting my cheek. "Me. My Bon."

I look down at the baby, who's frowning at me, too.

I can't please either of these women.

"What is it?" I kiss her hand again. "What can I do for you, gorgeous girl?"

"Me," she repeats.

"Am I not paying enough attention to you?"

She smiles big, showing off her four front teeth.

"She's beautiful," Olivia says with a happy sigh. "Like, *stunning.*"

"She is a looker," I agree without looking away. "Aren't you? And you're being so good while I chat with Olivia. You're a good girl."

"Look, I said what I came here to say, and I know you're busy. I can see myself out."

The doorbell rings again, and Paisley looks up at me with her lips puckered in surprise.

"Yeah, you're cute," I mutter as I stand and prop the baby on my hip. I turn to Liv. "You, stay. I'll be right back."

"Oh, I can—"

"Stay," I say again with a wink to soften the demand. "Please."

"Okay."

I open the door and see Kelly and Jamal on the other side.

"Mama!" Paisley exclaims and holds her arms out for her. "Shit."

Kelly sends a menacing look my way when she takes her daughter from me.

"Not my fault." I hold my hands up. "Olivia showed up, and I'm pretty sure she's the one who said it."

"Right." Jamal walks past us, carrying bags of what smells like Chinese takeout. "Where is she? I want to meet her."

"Me, too," Kelly says, hurrying behind her husband.

"Come in, why don't you?" I say dryly and close the door, then follow them into the living room where Paisley is now sitting on Olivia's lap, clapping her hands.

"Babies like me," Olivia says shyly. "I have a lot of siblings and cousins. And this one is absolutely divine. Aren't you?"

"I like her," Kelly declares.

Olivia smiles softly. "I'll go so you guys can eat. It was nice to meet you. Especially you, little princess."

She boops Paisley on the nose and passes the little girl back to Kelly.

"If you think you're leaving now, you're mistaken," Kelly informs Liv. "You can't leave me outnumbered here. Besides, Paisley will be sad if you go."

Olivia glances my way, and I nod.

"You should stay and eat. You're welcome to."

And, damn it, I just want her nearby for as long as I can have her. I hate that I made her feel uncomfortable yesterday.

Jesus, I'm no creeper.

I can't make assumptions about her level of comfort, especially this early in our relationship—whatever that is.

The truth is, I don't know her well enough to assume that she'll find something like what I did yesterday funny.

And I feel like a jerk for it.

"Thanks. I could use some food, I suppose."

The fact that she agreed to stay gives me hope that she might give me another chance.

"I'll share my moo shu fun," I inform her. "But I won't share the eggrolls."

"We got extra," Jamal says. "Plenty for everyone."

"Bon," Paisley says, reaching for me. I take her and kiss her cheek.

"Vaughn's her favorite person," Kelly says with a smile. "I'll go get things dished up."

"Oh, I'll help," Olivia offers and hurries after the

other woman.

"Dude," Jamal says.

That one word says everything he needs to say.

"I know."

"Don't mess this up," he advises. "I have a feeling about her."

"I do, too. And I'm not trying to mess it up. I like her."

"She's not a bimbo," he says, keeping this language clean for the sake of the baby, who's resting her head on my shoulder and dozing off.

"I know that, too."

"Maybe you'll grow up with this one."

His comment doesn't even make me mad. I know what he means. That it's past time for me to stop acting like a kid. And he's not wrong.

It *is* time.

"We'll see how it goes. We didn't have the chance to talk much before you arrived. She might be hanging around to be polite because you and Kelly are here."

"Nah, if she were still mad, she'd have left. We didn't have to try hard to keep her here."

"I guess you're right. It's a step in the right direction, I suppose."

"Come on. I'll put the baby down for a nap, and we can have lunch."

Just as we both stand, a blood-curdling scream sounds from the kitchen.

The baby wakes up and joins in.

CHAPTER 6

~OLIVIA~

"*W*hat is it? What's wrong?" Vaughn asks as he and Jamal come running into the kitchen.

Kelly's laughing her ass off.

And I'm covering my face with my hands in horror.

"She—" Kelly begins but then dissolves back into laughter.

"Is anyone bleeding?" Jamal asks.

"No," Kelly manages.

I drag my hands down my cheeks and take a long, deep breath. "There was a spider."

"A spider?" Vaughn asks.

"Well, I *thought* there was a spider," I clarify. "But it wasn't a spider, after all."

"That's how you react when you think you see an insect?" Jamal inquires.

"Doesn't everyone?" I counter. "It was *massive.*"

"And imaginary," Vaughn adds.

"There was a shadow from something outside, and it looked like a big, hairy spider running on the countertop." I shudder at the thought.

"But, to be clear," Jamal says as he passes the baby to Kelly, who has managed to get herself under control, "it was a fictitious spider."

I narrow my eyes at him. "Yes."

I like these people so much. They're not only absolutely *gorgeous* with the sweetest baby ever but they're also welcoming and kind.

And, because of them, I'm seeing an all-new side of Vaughn.

"Now that we're all awake," Vaughn says and smiles at me softly, rubbing his hand over the center of my back, "I'm starving."

"I'm going to put her down for a nap," Kelly says. "You guys go ahead. I'll be right back."

"How old is Paisley?" I ask Jamal, who looks *very* familiar to me; I just can't place where I know him from.

"She's just over a year," he says.

"She's absolutely gorgeous," I reply. "But you know that already."

"I don't mind hearing it."

We've just filled some plates with food when Kelly returns and joins us. "She didn't put up a fight at all. Baby girl was bushed."

"We played quite a lot," Vaughn replies with a proud

smile. "We played kitchen and made a gourmet meal. That'll wear a person out."

Yesterday, I never would have thought that Vaughn was *this* person. Sweet with babies and easygoing.

I'm so glad I decided to come over here.

"What do you do, Jamal? You look so familiar to me, but I can't put my finger on it."

"Football," he replies and bites into an egg roll. "I play for Seattle."

There it is.

I nod and snap my fingers. "That's where I know you from."

"Do you watch football?" Kelly asks.

"Yeah, it's sort of a religion in my family."

My uncle Will is a football icon, but there's no need to mention that here. I like that Vaughn doesn't associate me with my father. He knows me as *me* and seems to like me just fine.

I want to keep it that way.

"Well, maybe you and Vaughn can join me at a game sometime soon," Kelly offers. "It would be fun and a nice distraction because I'm always afraid my baby's gonna get hurt."

My family has a box at the stadium, but I just smile and nod. "I love to go to the home games. I'm always up for that. But you don't have to worry about him. He's a strong receiver and a fast runner."

"I like her," Kelly says, pointing at me with her fork.

"I do, too," Vaughn murmurs. He's sitting across

from me and has been silently eating, listening to us. His green eyes are intent on mine, but he looks relaxed. "I didn't realize you were a football fan."

"We've known each other for less than a week," I remind him. "I'd say there's still an ocean-sized number of things we don't know about each other."

"Jamal and I have been married for five years," Kelly says. "And I feel like I learn new things about him all the time."

"Only good things, though. Right, baby doll?"

"Mostly good," Kelly says and blows her husband a kiss. "So, you're a costume designer, Olivia? That's interesting."

"And fun," I reply with a smile. "I've been sewing clothes since I was a kid. I love fashion. And by the time I was in high school, I knew that I wanted to work with costumes for movies rather than be in high fashion."

"From what I hear, you have a very promising career ahead of you," Kelly says. "I might have asked around a bit."

"Thanks." I set my empty plate aside. "It's exhausting, but my staff is talented and eager. I get to meet a lot of interesting people. Not to mention, the projects themselves aren't boring in the least. The one I'm working on with Vaughn is a period piece."

"I know. I'm Vaughn's assistant."

"I wondered," I reply and then continue at Kelly's

raised brow. "I saw a photo of the two of you last night. My roommate came across it."

"And you thought I'd been out with someone last night after you stood me up?"

I nod thoughtfully and then say, "Yes, actually. I did. Kelly's gorgeous, and Jamal wasn't anywhere in sight in the photo."

"Fucking paps," Vaughn mutters and then looks at the couple. "The baby's asleep so I can swear."

I should have known better last night. My dad drilled it into my head for my entire life—the paparazzi lie and spin stories to fit their narrative.

I know better than to jump to conclusions.

"I *really* like her," Kelly repeats with a smile.

"How long have you worked for Vaughn?" I ask, changing the subject.

"Several years now. He'd fall apart without me."

"It's true," Vaughn agrees.

We spend the next hour just hanging out and enjoying each other's company. I learn that Vaughn and Jamal have been friends since they were kids and that he's closer to this couple than he is with most of his family.

And it only makes me want to ask more. But I don't. Not now, anyway.

"Baby's awake," Kelly says with a sigh. "Man, it was nice to have an adult conversation. It's been a little while. I'll go get her, and then we should probably go."

She leaves the room, and Jamal watches her walk

away. "She works damn hard between our little sugar pie and all of the other work. She needs to get out more. Have more fun. We have the part-time nanny, and she's great, but my girl needs a *real* break."

"My cousins and I have some fun get-togethers," I reply. "I'll invite Kelly to join us next time. It's a lot of fun."

"We're ready to go, Daddy," Kelly announces as she and Paisley return. The baby has a little crease in her cheek from the bedding and that I'm-not-awake-yet stare happening.

It's completely adorable.

"We'll see you later. It was nice to meet you, Olivia," Jamal says and shakes my hand. Once they've buckled the baby in the car and driven off, Vaughn turns to me and links our fingers.

"I think it's time we talked," he says.

"Me, too."

He doesn't lead me to the living room but rather out the sliding glass doors to a beautiful terrace that overlooks the pool area.

I'm a sucker for a pool area.

The Seattle summer is still hanging on by the skin of its teeth—if summer had teeth—and it's a lovely, warm day. I know the rainy season will settle in soon enough, so I'm happy to enjoy the nice weather.

Before Vaughn can even speak, I start in.

"I didn't even know that this guy existed," I begin and gesture to him. "I realize I don't know you well, but this kind, sweet, funny man hasn't been around at all since I first met you. The way you are today? That's sexy, Vaughn. You're sweet with that baby and at ease with your friends. I like *him.*

"I admit, I've felt the chemistry between us since our first meeting, but I don't like the arrogant, cocksure jerk you seem to portray to the world. It's a mask, and it's fake, and I don't like *him* at all."

"I just—"

"I'm not done." He raises his eyebrows but closes his mouth. "I understand that you have a public image—I understand it better than you know. But I'm not interested in that surface person, even if it's just a physical relationship. It's just not what I want in my life."

"Understood," he says quietly. "It's habit. I've put up walls for reasons."

"Like I said, I get it. But if that's the person I get to be around, the one behind the walls? I don't want any part of it."

"That's not what I want, either," he admits. "Just like I wouldn't want that from you."

"No. You wouldn't."

He's still standing, his hands in his pockets, watching me. My fingers itch to dive into his hair. It's been hard to be here with him and not touch him. But I couldn't while the others were here.

Whenever he's near, it's like static electricity consumes my whole body. I almost hum with it.

It's the craziest sensation.

"Come here," he says quietly.

I can't do anything but comply.

I prowl to him, enjoying how his green eyes darken as I approach.

His hands don't come out of his pockets as I drag mine up his chest to his neck and, finally, into his thick, soft hair.

He frees his hands and easily lifts me into his arms. With his eyes on mine, he walks into the house, up a wide staircase, and into what I assume is his bedroom.

"No kitchen counter?"

"Later." His lips tip up into a smile. "I've been dreaming about getting you in my bed, and that's where I'll have you."

"I'm not complaining."

His lips descend on mine in a hot promise of what's to come. Not hard and frenzied but hot and *needy*.

Like having me here, under him, is the only thing in the world that he needs in this moment.

It could make a girl drunk.

He gently brushes my hair off my cheek and lazily dances his fingertips over my skin, setting me on fire.

I arch against him, and he groans.

I slide my leg over his, and he takes a long, deep breath.

"I'm trying to go slow, to make this last, but you're not making it easy."

"I *have* to touch you," I murmur and drag my finger over his bottom lip. "Why do you think that is?"

"I don't care why," he says and kisses my fingertip. "I only care that you're here. You hurt my feelings yesterday, and that doesn't happen often these days."

"I'm sorry," I reply honestly. "I really am. And, likewise."

"Now we know what *not* to do." He sinks in to kiss me some more, and it's like a tidal wave of lust, emotion, and feeling like it's *right.*

That being here with him is exactly where I'm meant to be.

We shift from lazy to urgent as we strip each other out of the clothes so rudely in our way, and when my hands meet warm, bare flesh, I let out a long, satisfied moan.

"I want you," he whispers before biting the fleshy part of my shoulder. "Jesus, I don't *stop* wanting you."

"I'm right here." My hands drift up and down his bare back. I'm beneath him, his elbows pressed into the mattress at my shoulders, and with his eyes on mine, he presses into me.

It's so much more personal. So much *more* than the first time in his kitchen.

He takes one of my hands in his, kisses my fingers, and then presses the back of that hand above my head as he begins to move.

Time seems to stand still. Nothing and no one else in the world exists except for Vaughn and me in this very moment.

And I know that I'll never be the same.

∼

"I HAVE TO GO HOME," I inform Vaughn an hour later. We've been lying lazily, watching the shadows of the day dance on the walls of his room.

"Just stay the night," he suggests.

"I can't." I sigh and look over at him. "I have room-mates, and they'll worry if I don't come home."

"Just tell them you're safe and won't be back."

I grin and cup his face in my hand. "It doesn't work that way. I'm keeping you a secret for a while. Not because I'm unsure or ashamed, but because it's nice that it's just for us, even if it's only for a little while. Does that sound stupid?"

"No." He kisses my lips. "It's just new to me. Usually, women can't wait to call *TMZ* to make it media-official —even if there's nothing to announce."

"That's not me."

"I know that."

I could lie here all night, so I make myself sit up and search for the clothes that Vaughn threw all over the bedroom.

He rises to his elbows and doesn't even try to hide the fact that he's checking me out while I get dressed.

Not that I mind.

"I suppose you'll be working all week," Vaughn says.

"I'm in the office Monday through Friday," I confirm. "And I usually work from home on the weekends."

"You need to live a little."

I laugh and tug on my shoes. "I live plenty."

"I'd like to spend some evenings with you."

My heart skips a beat when my eyes meet his. "I'd like that, too."

"Okay, then."

He stands and tugs on his jeans but doesn't bother to fasten them or even put on a shirt.

"You're just going to walk around like *that?*"

"No one else is here."

I blink at him.

"I'm going to take a shower after you leave. Although, if you want to stay—"

"I have to go." I hold up a hand, making him laugh. "I *really* have to go. You'll have to fend for yourself in the shower."

"Bummer." He laughs and follows me downstairs to the door. After a long, lingering kiss, I manage to walk out to my car, start it, and head down the driveway.

I see Vaughn in the rearview, his arms crossed over his bare chest. He grins when I wave at him.

It should be illegal to look like that.

"YOU HAVEN'T BEEN AROUND MUCH," my dad says as we wrap up our weekly meeting.

"What do you mean?"

"Just that. We haven't seen much of you lately. What's up?"

Oh, you know, I'm just having sex with a movie star every second I can.

I've seen Vaughn every day this week.

Of course, I'm not going to tell my dad that.

"I don't know. I guess I've just been busy."

Dad narrows his eyes on me. I'm not a good liar. Never was. This man can smell a lie from thirty paces.

And, right now, I'm sitting approximately two paces away from him.

"I have," I insist. "Nothing major or exciting. What's going on with you and Mom?"

"Nothing major or exciting," he echoes. "You know, you can talk to me about anything, right? Anything at all."

And here we go with the guilt trip. "Yeah, I know."

"I've been thinking about Christmas," he begins, and I laugh. "What?"

"Christmas is like, three months away."

"And with a family like ours, we have to plan ahead. You know that. Anyway, I think the entire Montgomery clan is going to Iceland for Christmas."

I narrow my eyes. "That's roughly fourteen thousand people."

"I'm aware. We've talked about doing something big with the whole gang for a long time. If we start planning now, we can make it work with everyone's schedules."

"Iceland, huh?"

"It's beautiful. You'll like it."

"Sounds cold in December. But okay." I shrug, kind of intrigued by the idea. "I'm in."

"Excellent."

Movement at the doorway has us both looking up, and my stomach jitters at the sight of Vaughn.

And then it falls to my feet.

"Vaughn," Dad says in surprise. He smiles and stands to shake Vaughn's hand. "Good to see you. You've met my daughter, Olivia."

Vaughn smiles, but his green gaze flies to mine, and I have to swallow the lump in my throat.

Shit.

CHAPTER 7

~VAUGHN~

*H*is *daughter?*

I've been boning my boss's *daughter* every chance I get?

Luke Williams is not just the producer of the movie I was hired to star in, he's also the owner of the entire production company. He's one of the most powerful men in the business.

I've admired him since I was a kid, and being hired for this job was a big deal for me.

And now I'm having sex with his daughter.

"We've met," I confirm. "Although, I didn't realize she was your daughter."

Olivia's eyes close, and Luke smiles at me. "She doesn't like to announce it to the world around here. But, yes, she's my kid. You must be here for a fitting, so I'll see myself out. Have a good day, Liv."

"See you later," Liv replies, and we stand in silence until the door closes behind Luke. "Um, hi."

"Hello." I pace in front of her desk and watch her. I know her body as intimately as I know mine. Her laugh tickles my dreams. Her lips are a miracle from God.

And yet, I just found out that I don't know her *at all.*

"So, you're mad," she begins, and I hold up a hand, stopping her.

"I haven't decided what I am," I reply honestly. "I mean, I knew that sleeping with the costume designer was a slight conflict of interest, but now I find out that you're my boss's daughter. That is for damn sure a conflict of interest."

She winces and bites her lip. "Why?"

My eyes narrow, and she shakes her head. "No, really. Why? It's none of my father's business who I sleep with. It's not like we're dating or anything."

That remark hits me right in the chest.

"I've seen you every day this week," I remind her.

"Yeah. At your house. We eat something, have sex, talk for a few, and then I go home. That's not *dating* by anyone's standards, Vaughn. It's not like I plan to bring you home to my parents one day. And even if I *did* plan to, I can't because he would have a damn fit if he knew I was seeing you outside of the office."

I've never had a woman hurt my feelings so much in my life, not to mention all in one week. If I had, I would have walked away without a backward glance.

And yet, with this particular woman, I seem to be a masochist.

"There's a lot to unpack here," I reply with a sigh. "If I've given you the impression that I don't want to date you, I apologize. I just can't seem to keep my damn hands to myself, and fucking you on the table at any of the fine establishments in Seattle would likely be frowned upon."

She opens her mouth to speak, but I keep going.

"However, I'm sure I can keep myself under control long enough to go out to one of those places for a nice meal, or to a movie, or hell, wherever you want to go. Let's go."

She closes her mouth and frowns. "I just told you that I *can't* date you."

"And why is that, exactly?"

"Because my dad would lose his mind. You didn't *recognize* me as his daughter because he fought tooth and nail to keep my siblings and me out of the public eye. No photos, no appearances. He wants us to live our lives away from that."

"But you *work* in this business, Liv. You could likely be up for an Oscar next year. And I won't believe you if you say you won't attend."

"I'll attend," she says slowly. "But I work under my mother's maiden name. We don't publicize who I am."

"That's bullshit." The anger is swift and all-consuming. "Your father is Luke-fucking-Williams, one of the most powerful men in show business. He's not a serial killer or someone to be ashamed of."

"I'm *not* ashamed."

"You should use the name he gave you with pride and take advantage of all the doors it'll open up for you in this business, Olivia."

She sighs and rubs her fingertips against her forehead. "You don't get it."

"Are you kidding me? Of course, I get it. My last name is *Barrymore,* sweetheart. My family goes back generations in Hollywood."

"Okay, stop being defensive, and let me explain this to you."

Yeah, my back is up.

"I *am* defensive about this shit. It took me a long-ass time to get jobs on my own merit, and not just because of the name. I could have changed it, but damn it, it's *my* name. And I'm proud of it. I'll wade through all of the bullshit that gets slung my way because of it. I have an addict for a mother, and my father will fuck anything that moves when he's not making movies. And, hell, even when he *is* making them. Their reputations are shit, but I've worked hard to make something of myself despite them. And you're being handed a pristine reputation on a silver platter and just thumbing your nose at it?"

Her face reddens, and she shakes her head. "No, that's not what this is about. Damn it, Vaughn, I don't want opportunities on a silver platter. I want to *earn* them. And I *have* earned them. I'm in this office because I'm damn good at my job, not because of my DNA."

I raise an eyebrow, and she shakes her head.

"You know what? I'm mad at you, and I have work to do. So, you can just see yourself out. We can have an adult conversation when we've both calmed down."

"Good idea."

But I don't walk to the door. I march straight to her, fist her gorgeous hair in my hand, and kiss the shit out of her. I may be mad at her, but damn it, I never stop wanting her.

"I *will* see you later," I say. "I'm not leaving for good."

She swallows and licks her lips. "Understood."

I nod and walk out. I'm able to catch the elevator and am in my car in a matter of minutes, headed toward home when my phone rings.

"Hey, Kell, what's up?"

"I'm confirming the dinner in LA for Wednesday night," she says, all business. "Your flight is scheduled to leave Seattle that morning."

"Okay. Listen, I want to take Olivia with me. Can you get her a plate at my table that night?"

"Uh, I can try."

"You can do it," I say briskly.

"Why are you pissy? What crawled up your ass today?"

I take a deep breath and then decide *fuck it.* I rehash what happened in Liv's office.

"Lord help me," I hear Kelly whisper. "*Of course,* she doesn't want to ride her father's coattails, Vaughn. As a *woman*, she has to fight for everything she's got in this business to begin with. But if she attaches her father's name to hers publicly? Everyone will think she has the position she does because of her father and not because she's a talented artist. I know that you had your own challenges with getting to where you are in this business because of who your parents are. And you overcame that. But imagine being a *woman*. You have no idea how hard it is to succeed in Hollywood as a female, Vaughn. I think that what she's done is brilliant, and if her dad doesn't mind, why should you?"

I pull up my driveway and blow out a gusty breath. "Because I'm an asshole?"

"No, it's because you just took it too personally. It has absolutely nothing at all to do with you. She made the decision before she even knew you."

"Yeah, well, I suppose you're right. I just got my back up and overreacted."

"And now you can take a deep breath and not be an asshole when you see her again. You didn't do anything stupid and break up with her or something, did you?"

"No."

"Good. Because I like her a lot, and I think she could be really good for you. Just stop taking everything so damn personally. The world doesn't revolve around *you*."

"Since you constantly remind me of that fact, I don't think I'll forget anytime soon."

"You're welcome. Bye."

She disconnects, and I just sit in my car, staring at the city below.

Yeah, I overreacted. I guess I have more issues from my childhood and the people I came from than I thought. I spent years in therapy and thought I was past a good portion of it.

Apparently, not.

Olivia is the child of one of the biggest celebrities in the world, but she never had to endure what that means—being followed, having cameras shoved in your face. Never having a moment to herself.

Her dad protected her from all of that. And if I'm being honest, I respect the hell out of that decision. I wish my parents had done the same for me.

So, although we both come from powerful forces in our business, we have totally different perspectives.

It's a breath of fresh air, really.

And after our talk in her office, I have a few things that I need to see to.

THE RESTAURANT IS empty because it's usually closed tonight, but I pulled some strings and got them to open a table just for Olivia and me. If she doesn't want to be photographed and in the tabloids with me, that's fine. I'd prefer that myself.

But I'll be fucking damned if she'll continue assuming that I'm just here for the sex.

Okay, in the beginning, that might have been true. But, the more I've learned about her, the more I want to spend time with her—and not just between the sheets.

Which is new for me.

I'm not used to romance. But, damn it, I'm about to learn real fast.

"Does this table suit you?" the restaurant manager asks, pointing to a table in the middle of the room. The candles are already lit.

"It's great," I reply with a nod. "Thank you again, Chris."

"It's our pleasure, sir." He half-bows, and then we see Olivia walk through the door. "I'll show the lady this way."

He walks to where Olivia waits and escorts her to our table, holding the chair out for her.

"Thanks," she says and meets my eyes with hers. "Isn't this place closed tonight?"

"Not for us," I say with a smile. "We'll start with the wine and appetizers."

"Very well, sir. I'll be right back." Chris walks away, and Olivia's eyebrows lower in a frown.

"Did you already order?"

"Since we're the only two here this evening, the chef

is making us something special. Five courses, so I hope you're hungry."

"I'm starving," she admits. "I skipped lunch."

"Why is that?"

"Because you made me so mad, I couldn't eat."

I sigh and reach over to take her hand in mine. "I apologize for that. I really do. I let my emotions get the best of me. The truth is, it's none of my business what name you use professionally or why. It's your decision."

"My dad has been incredibly understanding about it," she says quietly. She doesn't pull away from me but rather squeezes just a little tighter. "At first, I thought it would hurt his feelings, but the more he and I talked it over, we both decided it was for the best. I'm not the first child of a celebrity to go down this path, in this way. And he understood that I wanted to make my own way. Forge my own career. Yes, I work for his company, but I didn't interview with my dad. I got the job on my merit."

"I told you before, you're excellent at your job. Of course, you got it because of your talent."

"I almost didn't come here tonight," she admits. "When I got your text telling me to meet you here, I almost said no."

"Why did you come?"

"Because that's stupid," she says with a half laugh. "And childish. We agreed to talk it over."

"I'm glad you came because I can't eat two steaks and two lobsters all by myself."

"Fancy," she says with a wink. "And now I'm extra glad I came."

The server brings the wine with an appetizer of artichoke and spinach dip and a fresh baguette.

"Oh, my God. I love cheese," Liv says as she chews the bread and dip. "Like, *love*. And it always goes straight to my hips, but I don't care. I can alter my clothes if I have to."

"Cheese is its own food group," I agree.

"You don't look like you eat cheese. Or anything with calories."

"I eat plenty. I also work out and have good genetics."

She smiles and reaches for more bread. "My dad is an excellent cook, and he's always getting my mom to eat. It's not that she has any issues with food, he just makes sure she eats enough. And it's kind of sweet, you know?"

"They still have a good marriage? They've been together a long time, right?"

"Forever," she confirms. "And, yeah, they're solid. They're totally gross with the PDA. Kissing and hugging and teasing. But it's also kind of sweet. However, I will always make gagging noises when I come upon them making out, just out of principle."

"That's very different from how I grew up."

"I honestly don't know much about your family. Are your parents still married?"

"Yes, because they're both too lazy to file the paperwork and because of the financial shitshow it would cause. My father is fine with my mom spending all the money she wants on whatever, and she looks the other way when it comes to the women he screws around with."

"That's healthy."

"It's the least healthy relationship I've ever seen. And, no, I'm not terribly close to them. I was raised by two nannies, not by my parents. We just pose for photos maybe once a year."

"You had *two* nannies? Like, at once?"

"No." I laugh and pour us each a little more wine. "I had one—Roberta—from the time I was born until I was about nine, and she retired. Then came Helga. She was with me until I was eighteen."

"Helga sounds like a nanny."

"She was the best. I'm still close to her. I was to both of them, but Roberta passed away about two years ago."

Olivia's green eyes darken with sympathy. "I'm sorry."

"She was in her eighties," I reply but still feel the sting of her loss. "Helga's more of a mother to me than my biological mom ever was. Did you have a nanny?"

"No," she says, shaking her head. "I have a huge family with lots of grandparents and aunts and uncles. So, if my parents were busy, we spent time with the grandparents. Once in a while, Mom and Dad would get a babysitter if there was a function where all of the adults wanted to attend, but it wasn't often."

Liv sips her wine in thought.

"My family has always been fine with including the kids, you know? Don't get me wrong, all of the old ladies—as my cousins and I call them—get together a few times a year for their girls' night out. But we all like spending time together. In fact, my dad was just telling me this morning that we're all going to Iceland for Christmas."

I tip my head to the side. "*All* of you?"

"Yeah. Everyone. And that's a *lot* of people, Vaughn. I don't know the exact number, but it's easily several dozen. I think he's crazy, but he'll make it fun."

I can't imagine doing something like that.

"Speaking of trips," I begin and lean a little closer to her. "I have to be in LA on Wednesday for an event. I'd like you to go with me."

"I don't think that's a good idea."

"Why?"

She sighs. "Because I don't want to be photographed with you. And it's not because of *you*."

"No problem. This isn't a red-carpet event, and they collect phones at the door. It's private."

She blinks in surprise. "They do that?"

"Yes. Not everything ends up online."

"Oh." She drums her fingers on the table. "Well, then I suppose that could be fun."

"Excellent. But, Olivia, you need to tell your father that we're seeing each other. Because I don't plan to *stop* seeing you anytime soon, and he needs to find out from you rather than from someone else."

"You're right." She nods and sips her wine again. "I know you're right. I thought of that earlier today after you left my office. I'll take care of it."

I nod and then lean back when the server delivers our entrees.

"Holy shit, this looks delicious. Good thing I'm hungry," she says, taking in the steak and lobster before her. "So, what should I wear to this party in LA?"

"Whatever you want."

Liv cuts into her steak and rolls her eyes at me, which only makes me want to kiss her.

"What will *you* be wearing?"

"A suit."

"With a tie?"

"Yes."

"Okay, that helps. God, this is really good."

She shovels some potatoes into her mouth, and I can't take my eyes off her. I love the way her lips purse while she chews.

I love the little moan that comes from her throat in satisfaction.

I can't wait to make that sound come out of her later, for entirely different reasons.

CHAPTER 8

~OLIVIA~

"*A*re the old ladies here yet?" I ask Stella as I hurry to the doorway of our favorite lunch spot in downtown Seattle. Stella always waits for me outside for our standing monthly lunch with our moms. "Sorry I ran late."

"You're fine, they're not here yet, either," Stella replies and leans in to hug me. "Mom said they'll be here in just a few and to go ahead and get our table."

"Cool." We walk inside, and the hostess leads us to a table for four against the windows. This cute café opened last year, and we enjoy the sandwiches and desserts. "How's it going? What's new and exciting?"

"Nothing new and exciting," Stella says. "And it's fine. Work is good."

"There they are," Jules says as she and Mom walk to us. "And it doesn't look like we missed anything good."

"We just got here," I confirm as I stand to give my

aunt Jules a hug and then turn to my mom and hug her close, as well.

Mom's a little bit shorter than me and curvier in all the right places. Her hair is long and dark, and I have her green eyes. I've always thought she's the prettiest woman in the world.

"Hey, baby," she says and kisses my cheek. "It's good to see you."

"You, too, Mama."

After all the hugs, we sit and look over the menu and then order lunch with the waitress.

"I'm hungry," Mom says with a grin. "How are you, girls? I haven't seen you in way too long."

"I'm good," Stella says with a shrug. "Same old story for me. Work, work, work. But I can't complain because that means that I have a good job. I like it."

"And you're excellent at it," Jules confirms and nudges her daughter's shoulder. Stella is Jules's mini-me. They look alike with their gorgeous blonde hair and blue eyes. They're more often than not mistaken for sisters. "I'm proud of you."

"You have to say that because you're my mom," Stella replies but smiles proudly. "What's Dad doing today?"

"He's in the office," Jules says. "And he says hi. He also told me to remind you to come over for dinner this week. He misses you."

"I will," Stella replies.

"And what about you?" Mom asks me. "What's new with you?"

Oh, you know, I'm just having amazing sex with one of the most famous men in the world.

"Not much, really."

Stella's eyebrow wings up, and she snorts. "Right. Nothing at all. Same boring Livie."

I narrow my eyes at her as if to say: *"Shut it."*

"What's up?" Jules asks.

"I just have some big projects at work, that's all. You know Stella and me, we're a couple of workaholics."

"I was hoping there might be some gossip about handsome men," Mom admits. "You two work too hard and don't go out enough."

Stella bats her eyelashes at me, and part of me *so* wants to tell these two about Vaughn. If he weren't famous, they'd get a huge kick out of it.

But he *is* famous, and I just don't want to open this can of worms until my mom and dad are together, and I can tell the story just once.

I promised Vaughn that I'd take care of it, and I will.

Just maybe not today.

"No boys to talk about," I reply, and my stomach feels heavy with guilt. I *hate* lying to my parents. It's the worst. "What's going on with you two?"

"I actually scored a pretty big job," Mom says, and Jules lifts her glass to clink against Mom's. "I'll be photographing some women for a calendar. Women with disabilities dressed to the nines, all in black and white. Very Gatsby-esque. I'm excited because all of the proceeds go to an organization that helps women with disabilities."

"That's awesome," I say and wrap my arm around Mom's shoulders to give her a hug. "You're going to knock it out of the park. If you need any help with costuming, let me know. I'm happy to help."

"Really? That would be a lot of fun. *If* you have time. I'll be working with the women over the course of about two weeks, so if you don't have time—"

"I'll make it work," I interrupt her. "I'd love to help. Working with you is always fun."

"You know," Jules says as she takes a bite of her salad, "I'm so glad our kids aren't assholes and that we actually *like* to be around them. All of the kids in the family are good eggs. Not everyone has it as good as we do."

"You're not wrong," Mom agrees. "Our girls are good people."

I cringe behind my water glass.

I'm a good person who lies to her mother's face.

Stella gives me another look. *Just tell them.*

"Okay, I can't lie."

Mom and Jules glance at me with matching frowns. "What do you mean?" Mom asks.

"I'm seeing a guy. He's super sexy, and I like him a lot. We're having a good time together."

"Now we're getting to the meaty parts," Jules says

with anticipation. "Who is he? Do you have pictures? Tell us everything."

"Oh, there are pictures," Stella mutters, and I kick her under the table. "Ow."

"I don't want to tell you who he is."

"Why? Is he a felon?" Mom asks.

"Does he have face and neck tattoos?" Jules adds. "Not that there's anything wrong with that. Your uncle Leo has neck tattoos, and he's very successful."

"No, he doesn't have neck tattoos. I just...I don't want Dad to get mad."

I say the last sentence in a whisper. All three of them get quiet, and then Mom rubs her hand over my back in a big circle.

"Your dad's a pretty reasonable man," she reminds me.

"Not about this." I take a long, deep breath, and Stella nods her head in encouragement. "Okay, I've been seeing Vaughn Barrymore."

"Thank the baby Jesus I don't have to keep this secret anymore," Stella says.

Jules grins. "Attagirl."

"Oh," is all Mom says. "Okay."

"See? It's going to be a *huge* issue, and that's just silly. He's a really nice guy—once he stopped being a complete cocky jerk."

"And the sex is probably pretty good," Jules says.

"I likely don't want to consider that," Mom replies. "I take it you haven't talked to Luke about this."

"Obviously, not. I need to, but I haven't yet. Please, don't tell him."

"Oh, trust me, I won't. That's for you to do. I think you're underestimating your dad here."

"It's like ripping off a bandage," Jules advises. "Just do it fast, face the music, and move on."

"Easy for you to say," I mutter.

"Wait, I still have to keep the secret?" Stella demands. "Like, you're not telling everyone?"

"Not yet. I mean, it might not even last. It could fizzle out, and then there'd be no need to tell anyone."

"Secrets wear you down," Mom says. "I don't recommend it. But it's your choice."

"I'll talk to Dad. I'll come talk to both of you. Soon."

"I don't see it fizzling," Stella says. "I haven't met the guy in person, but based on the last week or so, it's just ramping up. You should come clean."

I think of Vaughn and the look on his face when I assured him that I'd talk to my dad. I could tell that it was important to him.

"You're all right," I concede. "I'll come over for dinner next weekend and talk to him."

"Good idea." Mom smiles at me and then looks over at Jules. "Are we having dessert?"

"Hell, yes," Jules replies. "I want to hear all about the hot sex Livie's having while I enjoy some chocolate cheesecake."

"I'm not going to talk about that."

"Don't be a spoilsport," Jules replies.

~

HE LIVES IN MALIBU.

Not the Hollywood Hills or the Pacific Palisades. Vaughn's place is on the cliffs of the Pacific Ocean down a long, gated driveway. The house itself is modern, with clean lines and lots of windows so you feel like you're on top of the water. The furniture is simple, the floors cold tile.

And that's the best way to describe it. Cold. It's nothing like his place in Seattle.

We just arrived in LA this morning and finished with the tour of Vaughn's home, and while he takes a business call, I'm on one of the vast balconies, watching the ocean.

I'm nervous about the dinner tonight. It'll be my first industry event, and I'm going as Vaughn Barrymore's date. It's all surreal—and a little exciting, too.

I've wanted to go to these things since I was a kid, but that obviously wasn't allowed.

And I'm not here with Vaughn to sate some childish wish. I'm here because I like him, I enjoy being with him, and maybe it's time to network a bit.

"You found my favorite spot," Vaughn says as he joins me at the railing and looks out at the water. "I spend a lot of time out here, whenever I'm here— which isn't too often."

I turn to look at him. "You don't spend much time in your home?"

"No, I'm usually on location somewhere, and I prefer to spend time at the Seattle house. It's more comfortable. I bought this place so I had a home in LA and for the investment. You can't beat Malibu real estate."

"I suppose that's true," I murmur and brush a piece of hair off my cheek. Honestly, I'm relieved to hear that he's not here much. It explains the coldness of it.

It's not a home.

It's a place to stay now and again.

"When do we have to leave for the event?" I ask him.

"In about four hours."

"I should already be getting ready."

Vaughn laughs and then looks over at me in surprise. "Wait, really?"

"It's a process, Vaughn. And I have to sew myself into part of my dress."

"Hold up." He faces me fully now, interest written all over his ridiculously handsome face. "You have to *sew it on*?"

"It's a perk of designing the dress," I reply and lean in to kiss his nose. "It fits me like it was made for me. Because it was."

"You're going to kill me, aren't you? No, you're going to send me to prison because I'm going to have to kill every single asshole there tonight for staring at you."

"Oh, I think you're safe. I'm sure there will be plenty

of gorgeous starlets there for all of the assholes to gawk at."

He shakes his head, then licks his lips. "No one prettier than you."

I bark out a laugh. "Right. You're sweet. I really should go get in the shower and get this show on the road."

"Now, I can get behind a shower," he says slowly, thinking it over. "Make sure you get all the nooks and crannies clean."

"You stay away from my nooks and crannies," I warn him and then laugh when he swings me over his shoulder and hauls me through the house to his bedroom suite. "I mean it, Vaughn, we don't have time for this."

"We'll make time," he says, and without setting me on my feet, reaches into the ginormous shower to turn on the water. "This is important work. I take my job very seriously."

"No one hired you for this," I say with a laugh and then squeal when he sets me down and starts to strip me out of my clothes. "I don't have any of my things in here yet."

"You didn't unpack?" he asks and then clicks his tongue. "See, you do need me. It's a good thing I have a fully stocked bathroom."

"You're going to make me do all of this twice, aren't you?"

"Maybe three times, if you're lucky."

"We're going to be late."

"Isn't that expected?" He nips at my shoulder, my neck, and then leads me into the hot spray that seems to be coming from at least six showerheads.

As quickly as a snap of fingers, we go from playful to hot and all-consuming. Vaughn's hands roam over my wet body, his mouth covers mine, and it's as if the god of lust has possessed us as he pins me against the cold tile, lifts me, and sinks into me.

"God, I can't get enough," he says breathlessly against my mouth. "I never stop wanting you."

"Oh, God." I hold on and ride the wave of desperation coming off him. His muscles flex and move under my hands, and with our mouths fused, we both come apart.

Hard and loud in the echoing shower, we succumb to the lust that never seems to fade when we're together.

"Jesus," he whispers and then kisses my cheek, gently lowering me to my feet. "You okay?"

"As soon as I can feel my legs again, I'll be great."

He chuckles and then swallows. "I'm here, in case you fall."

"It should only take an hour or so."

He laughs again and kisses my forehead. "You're amazing."

"And I'm going to be *very* late now, but that's okay. I need my stuff."

"I can get it. Just tell me where to look."

"The suitcase is open on the bed. It's a red travel case. The others are makeup and such."

"You're quite organized, aren't you?"

"To a fault," I agree as he steps out and reaches for a towel before hurrying away. Less than a minute later, he's back with the case I need.

"You've got this whole suite to yourself," he informs me. "I'll be down the hall in a guest suite getting ready, but I have a couple of hours before I have to start. If you need me, I'll be in my office downstairs."

"Thank you. Really. I'm already having a great time."

His smile is quick and genuine. "Me, too. Holler if you need me."

It takes half an hour just to shower, with all of the shaving and washing and conditioning. I even use a pumice stone on my feet. I want to be sleek and smooth everywhere for tonight.

Two hours later, my hair and makeup are done, and I'm video chatting with Stella.

"Your brows are *incredible*," she informs me. "How do you get them so perfect?"

"It took four tries," I reply. "I've never taken this long to get ready for anything in my life, Stel."

"Totally worth it," she reminds me. Stella is the only one who knows where I am and who I'm with. "I know I wasn't completely sold at first, but you're going to have *so* much fun, friend."

"I hope so. I mean, I already am, so I don't see why I won't later."

"Just don't get jealous when other hot girls hug your man and stuff. Because they probably will. But you have nothing to worry about. I've seen the dress, and it's ridiculously gorgeous. You'll probably get hit on a lot."

"No, I won't, but you're sweet for saying so. I have about an hour to get into this dress."

"Didn't you overbudget your time?"

"No. I still have to sew part of it."

Stella frowns at me. "Why didn't you just take a dress that's finished?"

"Because I like *this* one. And I didn't procrastinate. It's supposed to be that way, so it fits just perfectly. You never know when you'll have an extra five pounds of water weight or decide to eat cake for breakfast or something."

"God, you're smart," Stella says. "I'm just going to hire you to follow me around and adjust my wardrobe accordingly so I can have cake for breakfast."

I laugh and choose a lipstick. "I bet I could make a lot of money if I offered that as a service."

"Right? Not that you don't make plenty of money now."

"Well, that's true. Okay, thanks for chatting with me. It helps the nerves, you know?"

"Does Vaughn make you nervous?"

"In all the good ways," I assure her. "I'll see you tomorrow when I get home and tell you all about it."

"Every. Single. Detail. Every one of them, Livie, and I mean it."

"Don't worry, I won't forget anything. Okay, see you later."

"Love you."

I blow her a kiss and end the call, then turn to the dress hanging in Vaughn's enormous closet.

A closet the size of Rhode Island that isn't even half full of his things.

"Okay, come to Mama."

AN HOUR LATER, after too many moments of cursing and sewing, ripping and resewing, I think I'm ready.

This dress, every stitch of it, is finally done.

I only drew blood twice.

Which isn't bad, really, given that part of it was sewn while on my body.

I run my hands down my hips and give myself a good study in the mirror.

It's a mermaid silhouette in cranberry red. Spaghetti straps hold up the bodice, which molds to my breasts and back and down around my hips. Nothing else is fitting in here, I'll tell you that.

At my knees, the dress loosens into flowing waves.

I've completed the look with black Louboutin heels and a diamond necklace that my parents gave me when I graduated from college.

"Holy fuck."

My eyes lift in the mirror, and I find Vaughn standing behind me in a nicely fitted black suit, red tie, and a stupefied look on his face.

I turn to face him and hold my hands out at my sides. "Here it is."

He swallows hard and then steps to me. "I don't think we can go."

"What?" I look down at my dress and then back up at him. "Did I misread what I should wear? I just assumed since you're in a suit, that I should wear something more formal, but I can make some adjustments, take off the mermaid skirt and shorten it up to make it less fancy if you think that's better."

"The dress is…shit, it should come with a damn warning label. It's absolutely gorgeous. We can't go because I won't be able to take my eyes off you, and I'm supposed to give a speech. I'll fuck everything up."

Everything in me goes gooey.

"You're a professional," I remind him and cup his face, his clean-shaven face in my hands. "You're going to do great. I'm just the date. Besides, you're so freaking handsome you almost make me nervous."

"Why?"

"Have you *seen* you?" I counter and make him laugh. It's good to see his shoulders relax.

"I'll be the luckiest man in that room tonight," he says and kisses my cheek. "And we should probably go."

"I'm ready." I reach for my clutch, which only has

my lipstick, debit card, identification, and phone inside. "Lead the way."

"I hired a car for tonight," he says as we descend the stairs. "It's just easier. I don't plan to drink, but this way, I don't have to fuck around with parking."

"Makes sense. You don't drink at these things?"

"I don't, no. I like to stay in control. Although cameras aren't allowed, you just never know who's listening or watching, and I like that I have a pretty decent reputation in this business—despite my parents."

"I can see that," I say and smile at the driver, who opens the limo door for us. "Thank you."

"Miss," he says and tips his hat. "Sir."

The drive to the venue takes almost an hour, but I don't mind, as I enjoy looking out the window at everything passing by. Vaughn points out landmarks and tells me stories of memories of the city.

When we arrive, I see that Vaughn was right. No paparazzi wait with cameras poised as we exit the car —no red carpet. In fact, it looks as if we're entering from the rear of the building.

I take Vaughn's offered hand, and he lifts mine to his lips, kissing my knuckles.

"I told you," he says softly. "This is a private dinner honoring Christian Wolfe. He is a fiercely private man. He wouldn't have allowed a big show."

"My family knows him," I say with a smile. "How lovely that they're honoring him."

We walk down a little hallway. Before we enter the ballroom, a young woman in uniform collects our phones.

"Don't worry," she says with a smile. "These are labeled and safely locked away. They'll be here when you're ready to go."

We're not late, but we're clearly one of the last few to arrive. The room is bustling with people, all dressed to the nines, mingling and talking.

"Oh, gosh," I whisper and take a deep breath.

Vaughn squeezes my hand and kisses it again. "Don't worry. I've got you."

And then the array of people swallows us.

"Vaughn! Darling, it's so good to see you!"

"Vaughn, over here, babe!"

So many people call out to him, wave, or smile. It's clear that he's well-liked in this room and among the most famous.

Vaughn never drops my hand and is sure to introduce me to everyone as Olivia Conner. I've never been given the side-eye so much in my life.

Stella and I will laugh about this tomorrow.

"I think that woman just grabbed your ass," I whisper to Vaughn as we make our way to our table.

"It happens," he whispers back, and I can't help but laugh. How can I possibly get jealous when it's all just so ridiculous?

"Vaughn, thank you for coming," Christian Wolfe

says as he stands and shakes Vaughn's hand. He glances at me and then does a double-take. "Liv?"

"Hi, Christian." He comes around to kiss my cheek, and the fifteen-year-old in me swoons just a little. I've known him for a long time, but he's still the super-hot movie star to me. "I'm Olivia Conner tonight."

Christian blinks in surprise. "Your dad?"

I just shake my head and turn to Christian's wife, Jenna. "It's so nice to see you."

"My darling girl, that is a *divine* dress. Tell me you designed it."

"Guilty." I laugh with her, and we take our seats. "When Vaughn invited me to join him tonight, I didn't realize that it was a dinner to honor your husband. Now, I'm even *more* excited to be here."

"How do you know each other?" Vaughn asks as he and Christian also take their seats.

"Our family has spent a little time in Montana, where Jenna's from," I reply with a smile. "And, of course, Dad worked with Christian quite often."

"We're getting looks," Jenna points out.

"I'm pretty sure they're just checking out the men. I mean, look at them."

So, we do. Vaughn looks as if he stepped out of a movie in that dark suit, with his brown hair perfectly styled. And Christian is drop-dead gorgeous himself, even if he is at least ten years older than Vaughn.

"Okay, I admit, our guys are handsome," Jenna says

with a smile. "But I think everyone's trying to figure out who Vaughn's date is."

"Olivia Conner, costume designer," I reply honestly. "That's exactly who I am. I've worked with some of the actors here. They'll spread the word, I'm sure."

"That was," I begin after we're cozied up in the limo on our way home, "so fun."

"You are a rock star," Vaughn says and kisses my forehead. I kicked off my shoes as soon as we got into the car, and I'm leaning against him, my head on his shoulder. "You worked that room as if you'd been doing it all your life."

"It's just about being polite," I reply. "I know how to do that. And it was kind of nice when some of them said they'd noticed my work. And I got to see some other actors I've worked with before. It's nice to feel like you're with your peers, you know?"

"Yep. I get it. No one understands our world like the ones who live in it, so it's nice to get together and talk shop."

"I had about half a dozen women ask me to design their Oscar dresses for next year," I admit with a smile. "Of course, I don't have time, but that was pretty cool."

"When you wear your work, you're a walking billboard."

I laugh at that and snuggle closer. "Your speech was

awesome. I think Christian had a tear in his eye when you finished. How long did it take you to write it?"

"I didn't write anything. I winged it."

"No way." I sit up and stare at him. "You thought all of that up on the spot? The story about being on set with him, how he showed you the importance of being professional when you're at work, and all of the other stuff was just off the cuff?"

"Yeah."

"Damn, you *are* good."

He chuckles and links his fingers with mine. "It was nice that your dad recorded a speech for Christian. I could tell that surprised him."

"I wish my dad would come to more of these things, but he won't. He's never really told me why. He just doesn't like living the lifestyle."

My phone rings in my bag.

"Who in the world is that?" I ask as I fish it out and see that it's Stella. "Oh, she's probably just wondering how it went."

I don't accept the call but text her.

Me: Headed home. It was SO FUN! See you tomorrow. XO

I set the phone aside, but it rings again. This time, it's my dad.

I don't answer.

Guilt fills my belly.

I didn't ask Christian and Jenna *not* to tell my dad

that they saw me, but I hadn't thought they'd call him first thing after leaving the dinner.

Dad doesn't take no for an answer. This time, he texts.

It's a photo of Vaughn kissing my hand at the party.

Dad: WE NEED TO TALK.

"Fuck."

Vaughn says, "You didn't tell him."

"No." I swallow hard. "I didn't tell him yet. And, apparently, someone snuck a phone inside that dinner."

Vaughn sighs.

I close my eyes.

Fuck.

CHAPTER 9

~VAUGHN~

*W*e're quiet for the rest of the drive to my house. Even once we're inside, we still don't say anything as we walk up to the bedroom to change out of our fancy clothes.

"Do you mind helping me out of this?" Liv asks. "It's going to have to be unstitched."

"I'd planned on ripping it off you in the heat of the moment, but somehow, I think the mood is gone."

She sighs and rifles through her bag, coming out with a little tool before passing it to me.

"You just have to put the metal piece in the seam and give it a tug." She instructs me on what to do. Before long, the dress falls around her, and she catches it at her bust. "Thanks. And I'm sorry. Let me get comfortable, and we can talk."

She walks away. Without another word, I shed my suit and change into sweats and a simple, white T-shirt.

When she walks out of the closet, she's dressed in similar attire, but her hair remains in those wavy curls, and her makeup is still in place.

"You're mad," she says before I can comment on how beautiful she is.

"I'm confused," I reply honestly. "You said you'd take care of telling your dad about us, so I figured you had before we came here."

"I didn't have time," she says and chews her red lip. "I did see my mom at lunch the other day and told her. But I asked her to let *me* tell Dad. And I was going to."

"But you didn't."

"I chickened out, okay? I thought about going up to his office, but I was busy, and he was busy, and then I decided to just go to their house this weekend for dinner and talk to him then. I didn't think a photo of us would leak because you assured me that it was impossible."

She gives me a hard-eye stare, and I shake my head. "Nope. You don't get to blame me for this one, honey. I took you to a party that didn't allow cameras or phones. You saw it for yourself. I can't help that someone didn't follow the rules. I hate that it happened, but it's not a lewd photo or even a scandalous one. I'm kissing your hand. I *like* kissing your hand. And you were my date."

"I know." She sits on the edge of the bed and sighs again. "I know it's not your fault. It's *my* fault. I'm not embarrassed by you or us or anything like that. It's just…it's my *dad*." She hangs her head in her hands. "And he's a great guy. The *best*. But I hate it when he's mad at me, and this could make him mad."

"Why do you think that?" I sit beside her and pull her against me, kissing her hair. "I mean, I'm not the best guy in the world, but there are worse out there."

She chuckles, and it makes my stomach loosen just a little. "I don't know. Like I said before, he's never really told me all the ins and outs of why he feels the way he does about Hollywood. Or about being famous. But I'm going to sit down with him and dig into all of that because it's important."

"I'm sorry that he found out the way he did, but I'm not sorry that he knows."

"Same." She lifts her face to mine and offers me a small smile. "It'll work out. Right?"

"Of course. There's nothing you can do tonight, so let's go cuddle up and watch something on the TV for a while before bed."

"Okay." She stands with me. "I should go wash my face and brush out my hair, but I'll do that before bed."

"You looked incredibly beautiful tonight," I say as I lead her to a little room down the hall that I use as a TV space. "I didn't have to kill anyone, but it was close a couple of times."

"Right." She giggles and flops down onto the big couch. "I don't think anyone was paying me much attention."

"You'd be wrong about that." I sit next to her and reach for the remote. "You underestimate how gorgeous you are, Olivia."

"I come from beautiful people," she says slowly. "My parents are a striking couple. My siblings and I are all pretty. It's just genetics, Vaughn. But when I'm in a room with the likes of you and Jennifer Aniston and Michael B. Jordan, I'm just...*me*. And that's okay. But I'm so glad that you think I'm extraordinary."

"I do." I cuddle her to me and turn on the TV. I'd envisioned coming home and tearing that dress off her, getting her naked, and pounding her into my mattress.

But this works, too. This quiet time together, decompressing from a stimulating night around a lot of people that I barely know, and she didn't know at all.

She lays her head on my shoulder and drapes a leg over my lap, sighing contentedly.

Yes, this works just fine.

IT'S EARLY. Light has just barely begun to creep through the bedroom's window blinds. Olivia is wrapped around me, sleeping soundly with her head on my chest and her arm draped over my stomach.

After we watched an old comedy and laughed on the couch, Liv washed her face, and then we fell into bed, exhausted. We were asleep in seconds.

But now that I'm coming awake, I want her with everything in me.

I gently roll Liv to her back and kiss her lips softly. My mouth drifts over her cheek, her closed eyelids, and her forehead.

She shifts beneath me and mumbles, her eyelashes fluttering as she opens those green eyes and sleepily smiles up at me.

My hands are already gently roaming over her warm, naked body, pulling her from slumber into sexy wakefulness.

I roll back to my side, and Liv hitches her leg over my hip. Face to face, I kiss her, then nudge my way inside her.

Christ.

It never fails to amaze me that it never feels quite the same, no matter how many times I've had her. She's warm and wet, yes, but this time, it's...softer. Slower.

Sleepy.

Her leg hitches higher, and I reach down to cup her ass in my hand, pulling her more tightly against me with every stroke. Every thrust.

"Vaughn," she whispers before sinking her teeth into my shoulder.

"Yes, baby. God, yes."

I roll her to her back and move faster, just a little harder, driven by something so fucking primal and so *basic*, it's as though I lose myself in her.

Every time.

The room is quiet but for our sighs of pleasure, and when she tightens around me, when she lifts her hips and arches her neck, succumbing to her climax, I bury my face in her neck and fall over with her.

"Did you just purr?" I ask quietly when I can breathe again.

"Mm," she confirms and kisses my chest.

When I move away from her, she rolls over onto her side and curls up. I swear she falls right back to sleep.

God, she's amazing.

I roll out of bed and walk to the restroom to clean myself up, then make my way to the kitchen for coffee. It's the ass crack of dawn, but we have to be at the airport to take the plane back to Seattle in a few hours.

We have time for her to rest, and I don't mind lingering over a cup of coffee while she does.

Once my coffee finishes, I pad back to the bedroom and stand in the doorway, watching her. She's turned onto her back, her right hand up by her face. Her long, dark hair is fanned out on the pillow, and her perfect mouth is parted just so in sleep.

I rub my suddenly aching chest and take a deep breath.

Is this what it feels like to fall in love? I wouldn't know. I've never experienced anything like this before.

Lust? Sure, I've been there plenty.

But this sweetness? This tender feeling that makes me want to protect and cherish her? This is new.

I'm crazy about her; I know that much. She makes me laugh, and she makes me want to be better.

God, it's true. I'm gone over her. And I know it's irreversible. Now that I've found her, I don't plan to ever let her go.

"Why are you hovering?" she asks softly.

"Am I?" I walk over to the bed and sit next to her. "I was just watching you sleep."

"That's kind of sweet. Is that coffee for me?"

"Sure." Hell, I'll give her anything she wants. I pass it to her as she sits up and tucks the sheet around her.

"Where's yours?"

"You're holding it."

She sips and watches me with sleepy, green eyes. "You said it was for me."

"It is now. I'll go make some more."

"We can share." She passes the mug back to me, and I take a sip. "We have to go soon, right?"

"We have some time, but yeah. The plane is scheduled to leave in a few hours."

"Okay. I'll get all my stuff together." She yawns and reaches over her head in a big stretch, letting the sheet fall around her hips.

"You did that on purpose."

"Did what?"

I set the mug aside and tackle Liv back onto the bed. "Turned me on again."

"I hate to break it to you, but it doesn't take much to do that."

I grin and then kiss her softly. "You're not wrong."

"Won't we be late?"

"It's a private plane, babe. They can't leave without us."

"Good. Because I want round two."

"Happy to oblige."

She doesn't know that I'm doing this. And she might be mad at me later, but I'll handle it.

Because it's the right thing to do.

I should have done it before we went to LA.

"He's expecting you," the admin says with a smile. "You can go on in."

"Thanks."

I walk through the open doorway into Luke Williams's office, then stop short when I see that he's not alone. Calmly, I close the door behind me and then turn to the older couple.

"Vaughn, I invited my wife to join us. Natalie, this is Vaughn Barrymore."

"It's a pleasure to meet you." I offer Natalie my hand. While she shakes it, I can't look away from her. "Olivia is the spitting image of you. Which means she's completely gorgeous."

"Thank you," Natalie says with a genuine smile. "Come in and sit down."

"I mean no disrespect, but I'm nervous, so I think I'll pace a bit."

Natalie and Luke share a look, and I walk over to shake Luke's hand and then pace to the windows, taking a deep breath before walking back over to them.

"First, I need to apologize."

Luke's calm face doesn't waver. "What do you feel you need to apologize for, exactly?"

I might as well just get it over with. "I've been dating your daughter for a couple of weeks now, and I realize there may be a couple of conflicts of interest here. For one thing, she's working on the project I'm involved in, and for another, her father is my boss."

Luke crosses his arms over his chest. "People in the industry get involved all the time, Vaughn. Even while they're working on the same project. *Especially* when they're working on the same project."

"Yes, but their father isn't usually the owner of the production company that's fronting the money for said project." I finally sit, though only on the edge of a long, black leather couch. "Not to mention, you're someone I admire, and I've wanted to work with you for a long time. I should have come to you before I became involved with her. Well, once I found out you were her dad."

Luke raises an eyebrow.

"But I didn't because the chemistry is off the charts,

and I didn't think of it." I clear my throat. "Olivia didn't initially want to go to that party with me last night. I assured her that no one would take any photos of us because it was a private party, and phones were checked at the door. But clearly, someone broke the rule."

"Clearly," Luke echoes.

"Okay, you two are giving me a headache," Natalie breaks in and rubs her hand over her face before looking at Luke. "You, my love, need to soften up just a bit here. *He* came to *you*. Not the other way around."

"There's a certain way things like this go," Luke informs her. "I'm the father. I'm not going to go easy on him."

"It's true," I agree with a half smile. "If the roles were reversed, I would have punched me by now."

"See?"

"I know that Liv will be irritated that I came to see you without telling her. But she's nervous, and she doesn't want to let you down. I don't see how starting something with me *would* let you down, but she has her reasons. I'm not an asshole."

I lick my lips and reconsider.

"Okay, sometimes I'm an asshole, but not when it comes to Liv. She's freaking incredible, and I'm not going to intentionally do something that makes her uncomfortable. I'm more pissed than I can tell you that someone took that photo when she clearly didn't want to be public about us being together. I'll find out who took it. I just want her to be happy. And, frankly, I don't plan on doing anything stupid to hurt her."

"You're a celebrity," Luke says simply. "Simply living the life you do, the *lifestyle* you do, can hurt her."

"I can't do anything about the fact that I'm famous, any more than you can."

Luke shakes his head and shuffles his feet. "You're right. You can't change it. But that doesn't mean that I'm fine with you pursuing my daughter."

"So, you're against us being together simply because of my name?"

"I didn't say it was fair."

"It's ridiculous," Natalie mutters. "Because if you had the same rules for yourself as you do for our children, you and I wouldn't be together, either. And I seem to remember that you were unyielding in your pursuit of me."

"Like I said, it's not fair," Luke repeats and shakes his head. "But I respect you coming in here today to talk to us, Vaughn."

"At the end of the day, Olivia is an adult." I rub my hands on my jeans as Luke turns his cold, blue eyes on me. "And she will make her own decisions. But she loves you more than just about anything, and I know it'll kill her if she thinks she has to go against your wishes."

"Are you giving me an ultimatum?" Luke asks.

"Not at all. I'm just stating the facts."

"I do believe you're in love with our daughter," Natalie says with a smile on her lips.

"I haven't known her very long—"

"It doesn't *take* very long," she interrupts.

"I don't think you're a bad man," Luke says slowly. "In fact, I quite like you. I think you're a hard worker, an excellent actor, and I see you doing wonderful things in our industry."

"But you don't see me doing wonderful things with your daughter."

Luke rubs the back of his neck. "No. I don't. Like I said, it's nothing personal, but you're—"

"Famous." My mouth twists into an ironic smile. "It's never done me much good, you know? I hope you change your mind. Because I don't plan on going anywhere unless Olivia tells me to hit the road."

"And that's how it should be," Natalie replies softly. "Good luck, Vaughn."

I hold Luke's gaze as I answer his wife. "Thank you. It was a pleasure to meet you."

I nod and walk to the door, then turn before I leave.

"Maybe you should ask yourself who, exactly, you're trying to protect here. Because the woman *I* know is more than capable of taking care of herself."

Luke blinks, and I walk out, moving down the hall to the elevator.

I don't stop on Olivia's floor. She's not in her office yet.

She went home to settle in and then planned to meet with her parents later this evening for dinner.

But I needed to speak with Luke right away. I needed him to know that I'm not hiding this. Olivia isn't a secret.

I'm quite sure that she's the love of my life.

And I'll be damned if her father will keep us apart.

CHAPTER 10

~OLIVIA~

I sit in my car and stare at the house I grew up in. It's a big home in an established neighborhood not far from my current house on Alki Beach. This one is fully gated with two separate garages, and it's gone through several upgrades over the years.

The inside has expansive views of the Sound, many big rooms, and plenty of space to play, hide, or find a little corner for yourself.

I know every inch of it better than I know the back of my hand.

And for the first time in my life, I'm afraid to go inside.

I blow out a gusty breath, reach for my handbag, and climb out of the car.

"I guess I'd better get it over with," I mutter as I

climb the steps to the front door and walk inside without bothering to knock.

We never knock.

Only Haley and Chelsea, the two youngest, still live at home as they both finish college. They could live anywhere, but they like living here.

I can't blame them.

"Hey," Chelsea says from the kitchen where she's chopping vegetables. "You've caused quite the drama around here."

"Are they seriously super-mad?"

Chelsea pauses and drops some cucumber into a bowl. "I wouldn't say *mad*. I would describe it as tense."

"It's fine," Haley says as she joins us. "Chelsea is just dramatic."

"Tell me Dad isn't walking around here with his teeth clenched," Chelsea challenges our sister. "He never gets super-*mad*. He just looks like he's chewing nails. It's kind of scary."

"Great." I take a deep breath. "Nice. Awesome."

"They're in their bedroom," Haley says helpfully. "You know, like they do when they want to fight or have a grown-up conversation without us hearing."

"Perfect," I add before walking that way.

"Good luck," Haley calls after me.

I'm not used to having these kinds of conversations with my parents. Keaton was always the one who got into trouble, not me.

I round the corner to Mom and Dad's room and stop when I hear them speaking.

"Listen," Mom says, "you said it yourself. He's not a bad guy. And he came to you today to have the conversation about Liv. I think that's a sign of a good, upstanding person."

Vaughn talked to my dad?

"You know why I feel the way I do, baby."

"I know. But I also think you should open your mind a bit. You're so laid-back and kind when it comes to people, so this is unlike you. I don't think you have an issue with Vaughn just because he's famous. What's really bothering you?"

There's a pause, and I can just picture my dad dragging his hands down his face in frustration.

"I know his parents," Dad says at last. "They're not exactly the salt-of-the-Earth kind of people."

"Yeah, well, not everyone has the good fortune of coming from amazing families as you and I do. Like our girl does. You can't punish the child for the mistakes the parents made. You're better than that. And you and I both know that Liv didn't chase after this kid because he's famous."

"No, I didn't," I agree as I walk into the room, and both of them turn to me. "In fact, I'm seeing him *despite* who he is. And judging him because of his parents is a dick move, Dad."

His eyes narrow, but I keep talking.

"I'm sorry that I didn't say something to you sooner

and that you found out that I'm seeing Vaughn because of a photo. That wasn't right, and it should have come from me. I intended for it to."

"You asked your mother to lie to me," Dad says slowly. "That's the part that really pisses me off."

"I just asked her not to mention it to you before I could," I clarify. "You two are a team. If I were in danger, she wouldn't keep a secret from you for me, and you know it. I'm not in any danger. I'm just dating a celebrity."

"Same difference," Dad mutters darkly.

"I had a really nice time in LA," I say softly. "I got to see Christian and Jenna, and Vaughn was a perfect gentleman about introducing me to people and staying with me. I thought he was a cocky jerk at first, but he's not that at all. I think you'd like him."

"I don't *dis*like him," Dad says and shoves his hands into his pockets. "But I want you to be careful. Mindful. You may see your mom and me as old, but I know what it's like to get caught up in falling for someone—the consequences be damned. To be blind to anything but that person. Jesus, I'm still blinded by her."

"Okay, that's kind of sweet and…gross all at the same time."

Mom laughs and wraps her arm around Dad's waist, fitting herself against his side as if they were two pieces of a puzzle made for each other.

Because they are.

"I think that would be my advice to you, no matter

who the man is, Livie. To enjoy yourself but be aware of any red flags, and be smart. I *know* you're intelligent and that you won't sit back and take any behavior that isn't healthy. No matter what Vaughn's last name is, just be careful."

"I am. I'm not under any illusions that this is a fairy tale. That'll be Chelsea someday, not me."

"God, help us," Dad murmurs. "Come on, let's get ready for dinner."

"You're not mad?"

He pauses and then reaches for me, pulling me into one of his big hugs where I feel as if it's the safest place in the world, and he'd protect me from anything.

Because he would.

"I'm not mad," he says. "I'm not even disappointed."

That makes tears spring to my eyes. The last thing I ever want to do is disappoint my dad.

"I'm…concerned. But your mom's right. I'd feel the same way, no matter who the guy was—because no one will ever be good enough for you. You're my baby."

"I'm twenty-five," I remind him.

"You'll be sixty and still my baby," he says before kissing my head. "Come on. I'm hungry."

"Me, too."

When we return to the living area, I see Keaton has joined us and is washing his filthy hands at the kitchen sink.

"Do you have to do that here?" I demand. "We prepare food in there."

"It's a sink with soap," he says with a shrug.

"You have your fingers in grease all day," Haley reminds him. "I don't want to see that in the kitchen sink."

"Why are girls so damn picky?" Keaton demands and reaches for a clean towel to dry his hands. "All they do is *nag, nag, nag.*"

"I'm gonna slap, slap, slap you right into next week if you don't get out of this kitchen," Haley says and nudges our brother away with her hip.

The doorbell rings, and Chelsea hurries over to open the door as I frown at my mom.

"Is someone else coming over?"

Mom smiles innocently just as I hear Chelsea sigh.

"Did my mom get me Vaughn Barrymore for my birthday?"

Vaughn laughs, and I jump off the stool I'd just sat down on to hurry over to the door.

"I wasn't expecting you here."

"Your dad invited me," he says with a smile. "Hi."

"Hi," Chelsea says and fiddles with the ends of her blonde hair.

"Oh, for God's sake, move." I nudge her out of the way and gesture for Vaughn to come in. "We're just hanging out in the kitchen while the girls cook. Do you want something to drink?"

"Water's great," he says and leans down to kiss me on the forehead. "You okay?"

"Yeah. I'm great. You talked to them?"

His green eyes warm as he nods. "Earlier today. I'll tell you about it later."

"Come on, you guys," Chelsea says and takes Vaughn's other hand. "You can sit by me. I call dibs on Vaughn, everyone."

While the others laugh, I move to my baby sister's side and whisper in her ear, "I already licked it, so it's mine."

"Damn you," she mutters and then laughs. "I know, but it's not against the law to flirt. Vaughn's a total thirst trap."

I mean, she's not wrong.

"You've now met the youngest, Chelsea. You can ignore her," I say as we walk toward the kitchen. "That's Haley at the stove."

"Hey," Haley says with a wave.

"That's my one and only brother, Keaton."

Keaton doesn't say much as he approaches Vaughn and gives him the beady eye as he reaches out to shake the other man's hand.

Keaton's only two years younger than I am, and we're really close. He's protective.

And I never know what's going to come out of his mouth.

"Nice to meet you," Vaughn says.

"And it'll stay that way so long as you don't fuck over my sister." Keaton grins, slaps Vaughn on the shoulder, and then walks away.

"He's a caveman," I say and glare at my brother.

"You know my dad, of course, and this is my mom, Natalie."

"We've met," Vaughn says with a smile for my mom. "It's good to see you again. Thank you for the invitation to dinner."

"It's our pleasure," Mom says. "Livie told us that you had a good time at the party last night."

"It was great," Vaughn confirms. "Your daughter is seriously gorgeous, talented, and can work a room full of people."

"Just like her mother," Dad says and kisses Mom on the cheek.

"It was so good to see Christian and Jenna," I add and pop a cherry tomato into my mouth. "He was a little embarrassed by all of the attention, but it was so deserved. And when they played the message you sent, Dad, I think he got misty. You should have gone."

"I called him earlier in the day," Dad replies, waving off my comment. "And your mom and I are planning a trip to Montana to see them in a few weeks."

"Are we all going?" Haley asks. "I love it there."

"You have school," Mom reminds her. "But we'll go again soon."

"I knew that you two had worked together quite a lot over the years," Vaughn says, "but I didn't realize you were such good friends until Liv saw Christian and Jenna and got excited."

"It was nice to have someone else there that I knew," I admit. "I'm not exactly shy, but it was still nerve-racking. I mean, *Michael B. Jordan* was there. And Lily-Rose Depp. Deacon Phillippe. You know, *everyone*."

"Including Olivia Williams," Chelsea says with a grin.

"Olivia Conner," I correct her.

"That's dumb," Keaton begins, but I narrow my eyes at him, and he holds his hands up. "Whatever. None of my business, right?"

"What do you do, Keaton?" Vaughn asks my brother, changing the subject.

"I fix cars," Keaton says simply, and I snort-laugh.

"No. Keaton hunts down old, rusted-out vehicles and completely restores them into gorgeous pieces of art, then sells them for six figures."

Vaughn's eyebrows rise in surprise. "Seriously? What are you working on right now?"

Keaton shrugs as if it's no big deal, but I can see the pride in his blue eyes. "I have a sixty-nine Corvette Stingray that's almost finished and a fifty-eight Plymouth Fury that I'm going to restore to look like the car from Stephen King's *Christine*."

"No shit? I want to see that. I'm a huge King fan, and who doesn't love a Stingray?"

"I'm using Dad's bonus garage for the Fury. Let's go have a look," Keaton offers, and Vaughn immediately jumps up.

"Let's do it."

"I'll go hang out with the guys," Dad says with a

wink and follows the other two out the back door toward the garage.

"Now Keaton will like him," Haley says with a laugh. "If Vaughn wants to talk cars, you may never see him again."

"I want you guys to like him," I admit.

"What's not to like? He's *hot*," Chelsea replies. "Like, smoking hot."

"Stop acting so thirsty," Haley advises our sister. "It's not attractive."

"He's a thirst trap," Chelsea says.

"I hate that saying," Mom says, shaking her head. "Thirst trap."

"You're married to one," I tell her. "Sorry, not sorry."

"You know, I think I'll call your father that later. He really *is* a hottie."

"Ew," Haley says, scrunching up her nose. "How did you meet Vaughn, Liv?"

"He's in a movie that I'm doing costuming for," I reply. "And he totally irritated the hell out of me when I first met him."

I tell them all about finding Vaughn in my office and what a jerk he was.

"But you also liked him," Haley says.

"Kind of? I don't know. I was attracted to him. And then I saw him with his best friend's baby, and he's so *sweet* with that little girl. When I saw that side of him and the arrogant guy with a chip on his shoulder went away, I really started to like him more."

"It's probably a defense mechanism," Mom says as she checks the lasagna in the oven. "Your dad has that sometimes, too. It's a wall they put up because they don't trust people. Too often, people act like they want to be their friend or whatever, but it's only because of their name or because of what they can *do* for the other."

"I get that," I reply with a nod. "I would hate that. And, I was pleasantly surprised to discover that Vaughn isn't a big, arrogant, cocky asshole, after all."

"That's so sweet," Vaughn says as he and the other guys walk through the door. He's grinning, his eyes full of humor as he strolls over to me and plants one on me, right in front of my family. "And back at you, babe."

"Ew. No PDA," Haley says, shaking her head. "We get enough of that from our parents."

"Your dad's a smart man," Vaughn says.

"I might like him, after all," Dad adds with a grin. "Just a little."

"I'll grow on you. You'll see."

"He knew the difference between the three-hundred-fifty-cubic-inch engine versus the more common three-hundred-eighteen that usually came in the Fury, so he has my vote." Keaton eyes the lasagna.

"Impressive," I say as if I know what any of those words mean.

"It *is* impressive," Keaton replies.

"I'm going to talk you into selling me that car," Vaughn tells my brother. "I need it."

"We'll see," Keaton says with a grin. "I just started on her. We'll see how she holds up. There's a lot of rust on that back end."

"As thrilling as it is for us to talk about cars," Chelsea says, rolling her eyes, "can we please eat now? I'm wasting away."

"Let's eat," Dad says.

CHAPTER 11

~VAUGHN~

"*J*like them," I say to Olivia after the front door closes behind us, and I walk her to her car. "More than I expected to, honestly."

"Why?" She leans back against the car and looks up at me with those gorgeous green eyes.

"I'm not used to families." I shrug a shoulder and brush my fingertips across her cheek. "But it didn't feel forced. It was…easy."

"They're pretty laid-back when they aren't being completely annoying."

"I didn't think they were annoying," I assure her. "Even when Chelsea asked if she could have my babies during dessert."

She shakes her head but can't help but laugh, and I join her.

"Well, if you don't ask, the answer's always no, right?" she says.

"True. You know what I *do* find annoying?"

She cocks a brow. "What's that?"

"That I've never seen where you live. We always go to my place."

The worry lines clear from her forehead, and she smiles softly. "You picked me up there before we went to the airport yesterday morning."

"I've seen the outside, yes," I confirm. "But I haven't seen your *home*."

"You're right. Why don't you follow me over there, and I'll give you the grand tour?"

"I thought you'd never ask." I kiss her forehead and then walk over to my Mercedes. Shortly after, we're on the road, driving through a side of Seattle I've never been to. Not even ten minutes later, Olivia turns into a driveway, and I park on the street before joining her at the front door. The house is a decent size in a nice neighborhood, lined with normal upper-middle-class homes. And if I'm not mistaken, we're not too far from the water.

"Nice place," I say as she unlocks the front door.

"Thanks," she says with a smile. "My parents own the house. My mom lived here when she met my dad. She and my aunt Jules were roommates. Mom never sold it, and it's come in handy for the family over the years. Now, I live here with Jules's daughter, Stella, and two of my other cousins. But it looks like no one is home right now."

She leads me through the living room to the kitchen

and out back, where there's a nice-sized pool in the backyard.

"I love the pool, even though we only get to use it half of the year," Liv says with a sigh. "That building there is the guest house where Drew sleeps. And I hear that my uncle Will just bought the property over there, so they'll tear down the fence that divides the two homes, and we'll have a Montgomery kid compound."

I raise my eyebrows at that. "How many are there?"

"Kids? A lot. And most of us are in college or older now. The older generations want us to have a safe place to live while being out on our own. Drew's been looking for a place to buy, so he'll move out soon, and someone else will move in here."

"It'll be party central," I say.

"Not likely," she replies, and we walk back into the house. "We *do* have cousins' nights about once a month, and we drink and get silly, but none of us are party animals. We're just too career-driven for that. And we don't let the underage kids drink."

"You're a responsible bunch."

"Well, there was that time when my cousin Liam went streaking through the neighborhood and got arrested for indecent exposure."

"When was that?" I ask.

"Last month."

She shows me her sewing room and then leads me into her bedroom.

"Our next cousins' night is this weekend. We're

doing it Sunday because of schedules. You're welcome to join us. Just promise me you won't go streaking."

"That's a promise I can keep," I reply and close the door behind me, turning the lock just in case one of her roommates comes home. "I can't guarantee, however, that I won't get naked for *you*."

"I think you should promise that you *will* get naked for me." She reaches up and pulls the hair tie from her long, shiny brown locks and lets it fall down her back. "And I'm not talking just once."

"No?" God, she's seducing me. I rub my fingertips against my thumbs. I want to touch her, taste her *everywhere*, but before I reach for her, I want to see where she takes this.

"You have an excellent body," she continues and steps out of her jeans, pulling her top over her head before letting it fall to the floor. Suddenly, she's standing before me in only a black bra and matching lace panties, and it feels like my head might explode. "My sister is right. You're a thirst trap."

I grin and move to her, sliding my hands up and down her sides and then over the globes of her excellent ass.

I lean in and press my lips to her ear. "I'm going to fuck you, Olivia. Not gently. Not sweetly. If you want me to stop, say so."

"I'm not shy," she replies, and I bite her lower lip.

She fucking *purrs.*

The burn of lust that I feel for her always simmers

within me. *Always*. But now it shoots straight into bonfire mode.

I urge her down onto the bed and tug off those barely-there panties. I don't toss them to the floor.

I tuck them into my pocket instead.

"You're stealing my *underwear?*"

"Not stealing," I reply as I spread her wide and take her in. "Taking. I'll buy you more if you want."

She just bites her lip, her green eyes shining as I lower my head and kiss her thigh. My fingertips brush up her inner legs, and then I grip firmly and plant my mouth over her.

"God, yes," she moans. "So *good.*"

I lap and kiss, suck and stroke, all while moving my hips against her bed. Jesus, I'm so hard I can't stand it, so I reach down to unzip my jeans and push them down over my hips, setting myself free.

I pull up and reach for one of her pillows.

"Lift those gorgeous hips, baby."

She immediately does as I ask, and I slip the pillow under them, shifting the angle just enough to make her crazy. After protecting us both, I plunge inside her and watch as her mouth opens, and her eyes close.

"Look at me." I brace one hand against her throat— not to choke her but to get her attention—and she does as I ask. "That's right."

It's a fucking frenzy. I can't go slow. I can't be gentle. My body takes over, and I fuck us both into oblivion.

But just before she comes, I slide out, flip her onto her stomach, and with that pillow supporting her hips, plunge right back in and grip her hair at the nape of her neck.

"Yes," she sighs.

I lean forward as I ride her. Still tugging her hair, I speak right into her ear.

"You're *mine*. Do you understand me?"

"Oh, Jesus."

"Tell me. Say it."

"Yours." She swallows hard, and I feel her pussy tightening around my cock. "God. I'm yours, Vaughn."

That's what I needed to hear. It's all it takes to send me over that cliff and into absolute bliss. I pulse against her ass, bite her shoulder, and she milks me dry with every contraction of her core.

"You destroy me," I growl, still trying to catch my breath. "Just fucking destroy me."

She makes a little mewling sound in her throat, her face buried in a pillow.

"What was that?"

She turns her head to the side. "Same."

I grin and pull myself off her, surprised that I have any strength left in my body at all, then walk to the adjoining bathroom to take care of the condom. I soak a cloth in warm water and return to her. I gently clean her up—carefully because I know I wasn't gentle, but she was good and ready for me all the same.

"I should take a shower," she murmurs but doesn't

move to pull away. "In about twenty years, when my brain cells come back to life. While I lie here and recover, you can tell me about going to see my parents today. Why didn't you tell me you planned to do that?"

I toss the cloth into a hamper across the room and lie next to Olivia, holding her close to me and kissing her forehead.

"Because you probably would have tried to talk me out of going."

"I would have," she confirms. "You didn't have to do that."

"Yeah, I did. I saw how nervous you were, and you're not the only one here, you know? I'm right here with you. The right thing for me to do was to man up and go talk to your dad. So, I did it this morning as soon as we got back to the city, and I dropped you off at home."

"What did you say?"

I grin and drag my fingers through her hair. "A little of this, a lot of that. Basically, I told them that I'm not going anywhere unless you kick me to the curb."

She sighs and drapes a leg over mine. "It was nice to see you with my family today. I didn't even know that it was something I wanted to see, but once I saw you there, I thought: *This is great. If I'm not careful, I'll catch feelings over here.*"

I tip her chin up so she's looking at me. "You're just *now* catching feelings? You need to catch up, babe."

She narrows her eyes playfully, kisses my chin, and

then pulls away. "I'm going to take that shower. If you want anything to eat or drink, help yourself to what's in the kitchen."

"Do you want anything?"

"I could go for some iced tea," she says and then blows me a kiss before disappearing into the bathroom.

Here's hoping there's iced tea in the fridge.

I tug on my jeans and unlock the door, walking downstairs. The house is still pretty quiet, so I assume no one's here.

But when I come into the kitchen, I see a pair of boxers and hairy legs sticking out of the fridge.

"Uh, hello?"

Whoever it is bumps his head on the fridge, then grabs a banana and holds it out like a weapon.

"Who the fuck are you?" he demands.

I raise a brow. "Who the fuck are *you*?"

"I live here, asshole. I'll call the cops."

"After you shoot me with that banana?"

He scowls at the fruit, then tosses it aside.

"I'm Vaughn. Liv's in the shower upstairs. You must be Drew?"

His eyes narrow on me, and he props his hands on his hips. "Jesus, you're *Vaughn*? The guy in *Falling Stars*."

"Yeah."

"Now I *know* you're lying because Liv doesn't date actors."

"How do you know?"

"Because I'm her damn cousin, and I just know."

"What's taking so long—oh." Liv stops by the island and tucks her robe around her. "Hey, Drew. This is Vaughn. He's, uh, my guest."

"See?" I say with a smug smile. "Not lying. He almost killed me with that banana."

"Whatever," Drew says, rolling his eyes. "A text would have been nice. Just because, you know. Courtesy."

"Sorry," Liv says with a cringe. "Maybe you should wear more clothes."

"Why?" Drew gestures to me. "He's not. Anyway, I'm out of here. I just wanted a snack."

He opens the fridge once more and takes out what looks like a plate of leftover meatloaf and potatoes.

"See you."

Drew leaves, shutting the door behind him, and I glance over at Liv and grin.

"That was fun."

"Sorry," she says and then laughs. "I guess that happens when you have roommates."

"I guess so," I agree and open the fridge, find some iced tea, and then open cupboards until I find glasses to pour the tea for Liv before passing it to her. "Here you go, madam."

"Thanks." She takes a sip. "Help yourself to anything."

"Okay."

I walk to her, lift her into my arms, and carry her up the stairs while she laughs like a loon.

"I meant in the kitchen."

"Oh, you want to do it in the kitchen? It's a little risky with roommates around the house. But, okay."

She giggles some more and kisses my cheek. "You know what I meant."

"I have what I want right here."

I step through her door and lock it behind us, then carry her back to bed.

"Are you sure this is okay?" Kelly asks Olivia as Liv escorts us up to one of the posh, exclusive boxes in the stadium. "I'm fine with hanging out with the other wives."

"It's totally okay," Liv assures Kelly. "It's the family's box, and you're more than welcome. Also, there's a great view of the field."

She opens the door of her family's suite, and we walk in to find it relatively full and a little loud.

This is not a place where Liv's family comes just to party. They actually watch the games. Most of the stadium-style seats, although much plusher than anything below us, are full of people eating and taking in what's happening on the field.

"Hey, Livie," Will Montgomery says and kisses Liv's cheek. "You brought friends."

"This is Kelly Jenkins, Jamal's wife," Liv says. "And this is Vaughn Barrymore."

"It's a pleasure," I say as I shake his hand.

"You're the one I've heard about," Will says with a smile. "Be good, or we'll kill you. Hi, Kelly. I really like your husband. He's an excellent player and a nice guy."

"I like him, too," Kelly says with a laugh. "He loves playing for this ball club."

Kelly and Will break off to talk about all things football, and Liv turns to me with an apologetic smile. "Sorry about that."

"No need. He probably speaks the truth." She passes me a beer, takes one for herself, and then looks over the food offerings.

"Want some wings? A slider? Nachos?"

"Yes." She laughs as I grab a plate and load it up. "Half of the fun of coming to the games is the food, and this looks really good."

"It usually is," she confirms and then licks some sauce off her thumb. "Let's load up and go watch the game."

"Good plan."

We make our way to some seats with our full plates and beers.

"This is my uncle Matt," Liv says, pointing with her beer to a tall, lean man who looks a little scary. "And his wife, Nic. Where are Finn and Abby?"

"Working concessions," Nic says with a smile. "They have jobs here during the home games."

"Well, that's awesome. Abby's nineteen and in college, and Finn's only sixteen. They're adorable.

You'll meet them. And that's my uncle Caleb. And you know Drew, Caleb's son."

"Hi," I say with a nod. "How many uncles do you have?"

"A lot," is all she says as she takes her seat and sets her beer in a cupholder. I glance back and see Kelly seated at a table with a view of the field, still talking with Will.

She'll come and join us when she's ready.

"These luxury suites are nice."

"Doesn't Kelly sit in one with the other wives?" Liv asks.

"No, she has seats down with everyone else. Most of the other wives don't even come to games."

"What?" She looks clearly surprised. "Why wouldn't they? Meg was always here in the box to watch Will. I just assumed that they all liked to come."

"From what Kelly told me, no." I clean the meat off a chicken bone, sip my beer, and yell at the field. "Come on, man! You had that!"

"That ref's blind," Matt mutters behind me as the guys set themselves up for the next play.

The quarterback throws to Jamal, who runs for the end zone, but a linebacker tackles him from the side.

Hard.

When the other man stands, Jamal stays on the ground.

"He's not moving," Liv says.

I glance back to Kelly, whose eyes are pinned on her husband on the field as she slowly stands.

I look down in time to see several medics run out onto the field and hover over my motionless friend.

Shit.

CHAPTER 12

~OLIVIA~

"*I*t's gonna be okay," I mutter around the lump in my throat. I immediately dash up to where Kelly's standing, her hands clasped in front of her mouth as she watches the scene below. "He's going to be *fine*. They're just not letting him move while they check him over."

Kelly nods in agreement, but she's clearly scared. Her brown eyes are wide, and she's chewing on her lower lip.

And I don't blame her one bit. Hell, I'd be terrified.

"He probably got the wind knocked out of him," Will says in a calm, matter-of-fact voice. "That was a hard hit. He's likely seeing some stars, catching his breath. He'll be back at it."

After what feels like *forever*, they help Jamal to his feet, and he walks with them off the field, waving to the fans as they applaud.

Kelly breathes a sigh of relief.

"He's awake."

"See?" Will says and reaches for a slider. I've known Will since I was born, and he's never stopped eating. "He'll be great."

"Until he's not," Kelly mutters.

"You can't think like that," my aunt Meg says as she wraps an arm around Kelly's shoulders. "Being married to a football player isn't easy. I get it. You'll worry every week. But you can only take it one game at a time. Hell, one *play* at a time. If you constantly worry that he'll get hurt, you'll drive yourself mad."

"Yeah, well, I feel like I do that plenty," Kelly says with a brave smile. "He's my world. Paisley and I don't work without him. If he were to get seriously hurt—"

"He didn't," Meg interrupts. "And, for today, for this moment, you can cling to that and enjoy the rest of the game. He's a professional, Kelly. He knows what he's doing. He also has some of the best doctors money can buy working down on that field. He's protected. You have to trust him."

"Yeah." Kelly nods slowly. "You're right. And I do trust him."

"Good." Meg hugs the younger woman. "And welcome to the wives' club. It's not like anything else. If you ever need to vent or talk, just call me. I'll give you my number."

"It's definitely *not* like anything else. I'll take that number. Thank you." Kelly takes a deep breath and smiles at her phone. "He texted. Says he got a knock on the head, so they're monitoring him for concussion. He's out the rest of the game for concussion protocol."

"Good," Will says. "Even if it isn't a concussion, it's better to be safe than sorry."

"Wish someone had said that to you back in the day," Meg says, rolling her eyes. "Can I get you a beer, Kelly?"

"Yes, please."

"You got it."

I look down to see Vaughn watching us, and I give him a thumbs-up. His face is ashen. I know he's just as worried for Jamal as Kelly is.

He sits back down and rests his elbows on his knees, looking down at the field.

Caleb reaches out and pats Vaughn on the shoulder. I can't hear what he says to him, but Vaughn nods and then smiles at my uncle.

Caleb can be intense. He's kind of a badass. As a former Navy SEAL, he's the strong, silent type. His poor daughters had a hell of a time dating in high school because he always threatened to kill their dates.

The scariest part is, he could do it and make it look like an accident.

But he's also a genuinely *nice* guy, and I can see that he's showing Vaughn that kindness now.

I love my family. I'm *proud* of them. Bringing Vaughn and Kelly up to the family's luxury box was definitely the right thing to do today. I intended for it to just be a fun day, but it turned into so much more.

"Are you coming to cousins' night tonight?" I ask Liam and Lucy, who are sitting on a couch nearby, looking at something on their phones.

"Duh," Liam says with a grin. "And this time, I won't get caught."

"For God's sake, keep your clothes on, sicko," Lucy says, shaking her head. "I dare you."

"You're no fun," Liam says with a grumble. "It's not like I got jail time or anything."

"I want to come," my cousin Hudson says. "I'll be twenty-one in a month. Let me come. You know you're my favorite, Livie."

I grin at him. "Of course, I am. But we don't let the underagers come, and you know it."

"*One month*," he repeats. "And I won't drink. I'll just hang and eat and stuff. I can be a sober driver if anyone needs it."

Okay, the kid has a good point. "You can come, but you will *not* drink, or I'll tell Uncle Mark and Aunt Meredith, and you'll get your ass whooped."

"I'm not stupid," he says with a scowl. "And I have to work tomorrow morning. If I show up to the jobsite hungover, my dad will kill me."

"Exactly," I agree. "Okay, fine. Bring some salsa, okay?"

"Mom just made some," he says with a grin. "I'll swipe a jar."

Meredith makes the *best* salsa. "Cool."

"When can I come? I'm a cousin." I turn to Zoey, Erin's younger sister.

"In about two years."

"So lame," Zoey says with a roll of her eyes and walks away.

"She's nineteen," Will reminds me as he watches his daughter sulk. "And she's *really* good at it."

"I was, too, when I was that age."

"I guess it's a rite of passage," Will responds, and then we turn back to the game when we hear everyone cheer. "That's right! Get it, boys!"

Seattle scores a touchdown, and I return to my seat next to Vaughn.

"You okay?" I ask him.

"Yeah. Scared the shit out of me, but he's gonna be fine. I like your uncle Caleb a lot, by the way."

I look over my shoulder at my uncle and offer him a smile.

Caleb just winks back at me and pops a cube of cheese into his mouth.

"Yeah, I do, too."

"Pizza's here," Stella announces as she and Drew come into the kitchen, each hidden behind a stack of boxes. "I got extra."

"Keaton will eat one whole large by himself," Drew says.

"Like you won't?" Erin asks, and Drew just smiles and opens a box, pulling out a slice of pepperoni before taking a huge bite.

"That's a lot of pizza," Vaughn says. "And a ton of vodka."

"One thing we learned from the old ladies," Haley says as she lines up martini glasses, "is our love for lemon drop martinis. Especially on these nights. But we have plenty of beer in the cooler outside for anyone who doesn't want vodka."

"How many people are coming?" Vaughn asks.

"A lot," I reply with a sigh as I try to count in my head. "At least…a dozen? It's probably easier to count the underagers, who I heard are all going to my parents' house for a sober party."

"Not me," Hudson says as he walks into the kitchen, a wide grin on his handsome face. "I'm here. I'm sober. And I'll stay that way. You won't have to cut my balls off or anything."

"Good, because…ew," I reply. "There's all kinds of soda and stuff in the fridge."

I walk into the living room and study it for a minute. Drew and Vaughn moved the furniture so there's more space for sitting. Dining room chairs are scattered about. Some will just sit on the floor, which is fine.

"This might be the last moment I have you to

myself," Vaughn says in my ear from behind. He wraps his arms around my middle and kisses my neck. "You're fucking beautiful, you know that, right?"

"It's just jeans and a sweater."

"Beautiful," he repeats softly before turning me around and planting his mouth right on mine in a long, slow, easy kiss that has my toes curling in my socks.

"You can just stop that right now," Stella says as she hurries past to open the door.

I didn't even hear the doorbell.

"The party's here," Liam announces and hurries in, wearing silly sunglasses and a weird, old, button-down shirt that looks like something from the seventies. "Where's the beer?"

"In the usual place." I point toward the back of the house, and Liam hurries past me. "Keep your clothes on!"

"I have bail money," Lucy says with a grin. "I smell pizza."

"In the kitchen."

Over the next thirty minutes or so, all of the cousins filter in, drift through the kitchen for food and drinks and then move out to the pool since it's a nice night to sit outside for a while.

No one makes a big deal about Vaughn. They're polite and welcoming, but there are no questions about movies or asking what it's like to be famous.

They're just normal.

Vaughn visibly relaxes next to me, and then I lose him altogether to a game of beer pong on the patio.

"I like him," Josie says as she joins me with a lemon drop. We watch Vaughn and Keaton play for a moment. "He's really laid-back and not pretentious at all."

"Yeah." I sigh and then grin when he and Keaton start to yell at each other over a questionable call.

"You like him, too," Josie says and sips her drink. "Like, a *lot*."

"Probably more than I should," I agree. "But, I can't seem to stop it. And I don't think I want to. My dad's not thrilled, but he took it better than I expected."

"Luke's a teddy bear when it comes to his wife and kids," Josie replies. "I imagine he's worried more than anything."

"I know."

"Come on," Erin says, interrupting us and tugging on Josie's arm. "Let's go chat while the boys play that stupid game."

"The guys are outside, right?" Haley asks, looking behind us.

"We want to know all there is to know about sex with Vaughn," Stella informs me and passes me a fresh lemon drop. "You'll need this because you can't leave out any of the dirty words."

I scrunch my nose and then realize that seven pairs of eyes are staring holes into me, and the room is dead-silent.

"No pressure or anything," I mutter and take a big

swig of the drink. "It's…ridiculous. Like, crazy-good. I'm not saying I'm with him just for the sex, but it's a factor because the man knows his way around, if you know what I mean."

"Are the orgasms, like, abundant?" Erin asks.

"Fuck, yes." I press my lips together as they laugh. "Oh, my God, you guys. I've had sex before, and orgasms aren't exactly new, but holy shitballs, this guy makes it his one job in life to make sure I come *constantly.*"

"He's doing the Lord's work," Josie says, holding her glass up in cheers. "God bless him."

"Does he have a signature move?" Sophie asks, leaning in and gesturing with a breadstick. "You know, like a certain way he kisses? Or does he use his fingers in a particularly good way?"

"He pulls my hair," I admit with a grin.

"I don't like that," Lucy decides. "A guy did that once, and I was like…I'm not a horse, buddy."

"That's because he didn't do it right," Maddie says with a laugh. "Not all men can. You really have to teach them because when it's done correctly, it's hot as fuck."

"She's right," I concur. "If a guy just, like, pulls your hair into a ponytail and it's all flopping around, that's not sexy. Yuck. No. The trick is for him to make a fist in your hair at your scalp, right on the back of your head. Firm but not too hard."

Before I can reach up to demonstrate, I hear, "Like this."

Vaughn swoops up behind me and turns me around to face him. His green eyes are full of humor, his lips a mere inch from mine as his hand drifts up my back and he makes a fist in my hair in just that right spot.

He tugs, just a bit, and then his mouth is on mine in one hell of a kiss. I hear the catcalls and whoops around us, and when he pulls back and smiles down at me, my heart just simply stutters.

"Wow," I whisper.

"Okay, I think I like *that*," Lucy announces. "I'm next. Try it out on me."

"Not a chance in hell," I say, still staring up at him. He just chuckles and kisses my forehead, then pulls away.

"The conversation in here is very interesting."

"We wanted to hear all about the sexy stuff," Stella says. "And we're not sorry."

"Neither am I. It sounds…stimulating."

"Okay, let's play Never Have I Ever," Haley says as the other guys come in the room, looking glassy-eyed and rosy-cheeked. "It's easy and fun. I refuse to play Truth or Dare because that's how Liam got arrested last time."

"Drink refills first," Drew says as he marches back into the kitchen.

"And a pee break," Liam agrees.

For the next fifteen minutes, there's a little chaos as everyone fills up on drinks and food and takes a pit stop.

"I didn't know you liked the hair thing so much," Vaughn whispers in my ear.

"It might be the hottest thing you do."

His eyebrow wings up in surprise. *"That* is?"

I nod and lick my lips. "Yeah. Definitely."

"Honey, if that's the thing that floats your boat, I need to step up my game a bit."

"You might kill me if it's any better."

Vaughn laughs, and the others filter back in to resume their seats.

"You know, I don't think I formally introduced you to everyone. I'll go around the room real quick. Don't worry if you can't remember names later because it's a lot."

"Let's do this," he agrees.

I start immediately to my right. "You know Stella. Next to her is Maddie, and right over there is Maddie's twin, Josie. They're the oldest of us and are Caleb's daughters. You know their brother, Drew."

"Met him in his underwear," Vaughn agrees, much to everyone's delight.

"That's Hudson, sitting on the floor with a Coke. He's not quite twenty-one yet, but he's super close. His sister is Lucy, and they're my uncle Mark's kids."

"Hey," Lucy says with a wave.

"Haley and Keaton are my sibs, and you've met them," I continue, looking around to see who I'm missing, then point at Sophie. "Sophie and Liam are my uncle Isaac's kiddos. Who did I forget?"

"Just me, but we've met," Erin says with a smile. "I'm Will's oldest."

"And that's everyone here. There are five more, of course. Chelsea, Zoey, Abby, Finn, and Emma. And that's all of us." I take Vaughn's hand and link our fingers. "Okay, let's play this game."

"Me first, since it was my idea," Haley says with an excited grin. "Never have I ever been to Scotland."

Vaughn's the only one who drinks. "I filmed a movie there. And why do I have the feeling that I'm about to get really drunk? Maybe I should grab some water."

"We'll go easy on you," Liam says. "Maybe."

"Never have I ever been arrested for streaking," Vaughn says, and Liam laughs, then drinks.

"I like you," Liam says. "Okay, never have I ever captained a boat."

And so it goes for the next hour.

"Never have I ever had sex in a public place," Lucy says, and we laugh when about half of the group drinks.

Vaughn and I don't.

"Never have I ever sent a dirty text to the wrong person," Sophie adds.

I drink. Vaughn stares at me, and I giggle and shrug. "Oops. Never have I ever said the wrong name in bed."

Keaton and Vaughn both drink, and I slap Vaughn's arm.

"It was in a scene," he says, defending himself. "I

couldn't remember the character's name, and I called her something else."

"I don't think that counts," Stella says.

"Trust me, in that moment, it counted," Vaughn says.

"And what was your excuse?" Stella asks Keaton.

"I'm a dumbass," Keaton replies with a shrug. "Okay, never have I ever…"

CHAPTER 13

~VAUGHN~

"*I* think I have to take literally *everyone* home," Hudson says as he shakes his head at all his drunk cousins. As far as I can tell, there are two of him right now.

The room is a little spinny.

Drinking games are the fucking devil. I know better.

But at least there's no threat of stupid photos being released to the press here. And isn't that just a goddamn miracle?

"That's what you signed on for," Liv reminds Hudson. "In exchange for coming, you're the sober driver."

"Yeah, yeah," Hudson says as we help get the others all into Hudson's SUV. "I don't have enough seatbelts for all of you. If I get pulled over, I'm fucked."

"I think the cop will be grateful that you're getting

them all home safely," Drew says and claps Hudson on the shoulder. "You're a bonafide fucking hero, my boy."

"That's my boob, you perv," Lucy says.

"Did Liam cop a feel?" Haley asks. "That's gross."

"No, it was Sophie," Lucy replies with a laugh.

Good God, these people are hilarious.

Once the door is closed and Hudson's behind the wheel, he takes off, and I survey all the cars on the street.

"I guess they'll be back for their cars tomorrow?"

"That's how it works," Stella says with a drunk smile. "I'm gonna go to bed. Bye."

"I wanna go to bed, too," Liv says as she practically falls into me. "I can't see."

"Your eyes are closed." I wrap my arm around her and guide her back inside. "We just have to get upstairs."

"Easy-peasy," she agrees. "Maybe I'll sit over here and get my energy up."

"No, no sitting." I hold onto her and point her up the stairs. "You can do it."

"It's a core workout," Liv complains. "Climbing stairs. Did you know that? Why?"

"I think it's legs." I plant my hand on her ass and push, helping her up to the second floor.

"Legs, core, whatever." She giggles and walks into her bedroom. I barely manage to get the door closed before we both flop onto the bed on our backs, staring at the ceiling.

"That was a successful party."

"They usually are," she says and brushes her hair out of her face. "Thbthbthbthb. Dumb hair. Why don't you have hair in your face?"

"Mine isn't that long."

"Not fair," she says with a pout. "I think Stella was jealous about your hair pulling techni-tenic-talent."

I laugh at the way she stutters and slurs her words. "Why?"

"She needs a boy." Liv sighs and reaches for my hand, linking her fingers with mine. "She's so fucking pretty. Right? Don't you think so?"

The truth is, Stella is a fucking stunner. She's absolutely gorgeous.

But I feel like this might be a trick question.

"She's pretty, sure."

"Like, she's not just pretty. She's goooooorgeous."

"Not as gorgeous as you."

Liv giggles. "You're nice to me. Anyway, she's so pretty but even better in here."

She slaps her free hand on her chest.

"In here? She's just the best. And she should find a nice guy, one who doesn't just want to fuck her and be an asshole. I hate fuckboys. Don't you?"

"Despise them," I reply, adoring her. "She'll find someone."

"Yeah."

"Would I be a fuckboy if I told you that I want to fuck *you*?"

"No." She looks over at me and then closes her eyes. "Spinning. What do you want to do to me, anyway? Pull my hair?"

"For starters." Now that I know how much she loves the hair pulling, I'll never fucking stop. "I want to lick your belly button."

"Ew." She laughs. "What if there's lint in there?"

"I'll clean it first." I laugh out loud, totally tickled by that. "And I want to kiss down your spine. I don't think I've done that yet."

"I want to kiss the dimples above your ass," she says with a happy sigh. "It's just so…kissable."

"My ass?"

"Mm. And I want to suck on your cock."

"Okay. That sounds good. I'm going to kiss your nipples and finger-fuck you until you beg for mercy."

"Wow. That sounds fun. What about toys?"

"What about them?"

"Should we play with some? Like a vibrator? Oh! Do you want to tie me up, all red-room style?"

"Would *you* like me to?"

"Yeah." She scratches her nose. "That could be fun. But don't whip me or anything. I'm not that hardcore."

"I feel like I should be taking notes. Do you have any toys?"

"Just a vibrator that Stella got me for my twenty-third birthday a couple of years ago. I've never used it, though."

"Why not?"

She shrugs. "Dunno. *We* could play with it."

"Sure."

"But let's rest for a minute first, just to get some energy. Maybe make the room stop spinning. I feel like I'm on a roller-coaster."

"Good idea."

"I'm gonna close my eyes and rest them," she informs me.

"Okay."

She's quiet for a minute, and I look over at her. "Are you all rested and ready?"

She snores softly.

I grin at her.

"Are you asleep?"

No answer.

"Well, since you're asleep, I guess I can tell you this." I swallow hard and look back up at the ceiling. The room really *is* spinning like a motherfucker.

"Do motherfuckers spin?" I ask out loud. "Anyway, that's not what I was going to say. I love you, Olivia. I love you so fucking much it scares me."

I take a long, deep breath and feel mildly sick as if I might throw up.

Maybe it's the alcohol.

"Maybe it's love," I mutter. "I love everything about you, and I don't even know everything yet. You're so damn cute and funny. And I love how big your family is and that you love them all so much. I admit, they

183

intimidate the hell out of me, but that's just because I'm not used to it, you know?"

I glance over, expecting a response, but she's still sleeping peacefully.

"You're so beautiful; you steal the breath from my body." I want to reach over and touch her cheek, but I stop myself.

"The sex is crazy-good, but it's so much more than that. I can't keep my hands to myself, and I want to protect you and *cherish* you, and...man, if that doesn't make me sound like a lunatic, I don't know what does. I don't even know if I'm the one talking right now.

"It feels like I'm talking. Yeah, I'm talking. Talking. Talk. Ing. I've said that too much, and now it feels weird. Have you ever done that? When you say a word too much and then it doesn't even sound like a word anymore? Probably not. You're too smart to do that."

I sigh, and that turns into a yawn. Liv's bed is comfortable.

"Maybe you have the right idea. We should just sleep this off and play with your toy some other time. We have all the time in the world. Because I plan to marry you. Oops, I wasn't supposed to say that. Don't want to scare you away. Better stop talking."

I frown.

"Talking. What a weird word." I yawn again and turn on my side so I'm facing Liv. "Goodnight, baby. If you throw up, I'll help. Love you."

~

"WHERE ARE WE GOING?" Liv asks as I drive us away from her office building after work, headed toward the freeway.

"We're getting out of town for a couple of hours," I reply with a grin. "I know it's rainy and messy, but it's not cold, and I need some fresh air."

"Oh, God, are we hiking? I don't have the shoes for that."

"They're in the backseat," I reply with a grin. "Stella did me a solid. Don't worry. We're not doing anything too wild and adventurous. How was work today?"

"It was a Wednesday," she says simply, and I frown over at her. She's in a weird mood.

"What does that mean?"

"That it was just like any other Wednesday. Nothing much happening. Same old thing. You know?"

It's been several days since we got pass-out drunk at the party. "Are you still hungover?"

That finally makes her smile. "No. Sorry. I had vendor issues today, so I'm not getting the very specific, very *beautiful* fabric that I wanted for Adam's costume, and one of the girls on my team quit on me because I told her she couldn't take a whole month off work to go find herself in Tibet. I mean, she's a little eccentric, but she's a damn good seamstress, and now I'm down a team member when I'm tackling two projects at once."

"Tibet?"

"Right? I guess she wanted to climb Mount Everest and meet with the Dalai Lama or something."

"Are those things in Tibet?" I wonder.

"I have no idea. The point is, I couldn't spare her for a whole month, so that pissed her off, and she railed at me for not valuing everything that she brings to the table, and said I'm just a spoiled, rich brat and that the only reason I have my job is because I probably boned the boss."

"Whoa."

"And I said, *'Who in their right mind bones their father?'* And then she got upset and said that I only have the job because of my dad. I told her to get the hell out. And she told me she quit."

Silently, I reach for Liv's hand and bring it to my mouth, kissing her tense fingers.

"You had a busy day."

"Yeah." She sighs and then takes a long, deep breath. "I hate people sometimes. I'm so much happier by myself with my sewing machine. Unfortunately, in order to do my job, I *have* to be around people. For the most part, it's fine. I do have a good team. And yesterday, I would have said that Kelsang was a nice girl."

"Kelsang?"

"That's her Tibetan name," Liv replies and rolls her eyes. "Her real name is Lindsey, but as of two months ago, we were only allowed to call her Kelsang."

"Interesting."

"That's what I said. Anyway, maybe the fresh air will be good for me, too. Or I'll get eaten by a bear and won't have to worry about Kelsang anymore."

"Are there bears in Seattle?"

"I don't think so."

Roughly thirty minutes after Olivia got into my car, I take the exit for Snoqualmie Falls.

"Oh, this is one of my favorite places," she says with a smile.

"I haven't been before, and I heard that it's nice."

"It is. Good call."

Because of the later hour, it doesn't take long to find parking, and then after she changes into sneakers, Liv and I are walking hand in hand over a footbridge, past a lodge, to where the water flows in a violent rush.

The air is full of mist from the water and the falling rain, and Olivia and I are the only two standing on the wooden walkway, looking down on the falls.

I take in a long breath and smile down at Liv. "Yeah, this was a good call."

"Excellent call," she agrees and leans against me. "Sorry I was so pissy when you picked me up."

"You had a shitty day." I kiss the top of her head. "I'm sorry about that."

"It's not the end of the world. This helps a lot. There's a restaurant in Snoqualmie that's great. Are you interested in grabbing dinner?"

"Hell, yes. Let's do it."

The steakhouse Liv recommends is great. The atmosphere is casual, and the food is fantastic.

"Best steak in Washington," Liv says as she wipes her mouth with her napkin. "And I haven't been here in years. Did you like it?"

"Did you see the size of that ribeye? What's not to like?"

"So, you're not one of those stereotypical actors who only eats lettuce and drinks protein shakes?"

I laugh and shake my head. "No. I don't know anyone like that, actually. I do know some vegans, but most people eat balanced diets. Even them. Thankfully, eating disorders are mostly a thing of the past in my profession."

"That's good," Liv says with a nod and then narrows her eyes at someone who just walked past. "I think that person has been taking our picture."

"They have," I confirm and reach over to take her hand in mine. "Just ignore them."

"It's annoying," she says with a frown. "They don't even ask."

"They never do. The paparazzi are worse. At least fans aren't aggressive about it."

"Well, I'm sorry. If I'd known, I wouldn't have suggested this place."

"I'm glad you did. This shit happens, Liv. A lot. You just have to roll with it if you don't want to be a complete hermit."

She nods, and I signal to the waitress for the check. I pay, and then we walk out to my car.

Liv's quiet and reaches for her phone, starting to thumb through it. I know she's tired, and I hate that she had a rough day.

But I guess we all have them sometimes. I'll draw a nice, hot bath for her and rub her feet later. Pamper her a little. With some wine and TLC, she'll feel better.

"What in the actual fuck?" she wonders aloud.

"What's up?"

"I know you're driving, but this."

She shows me her phone, and I quickly glance at it. She's looking through Instagram, and there are two side-by-side images. On the left is a picture of me with another woman about six years ago.

On the right is the photo of Liv and me the night we went to the dinner party in LA.

"The caption reads: *Which woman is best for Vaughn?* And then they go through about ten points as to why they think this other woman, Adrienne McCoy, is a better match for you."

"Fuck."

"Among those reasons," Liv continues, her voice full of hurt and anger, "is because Adrienne has a great house in Hawaii, her father is in oil—whatever the hell that means—and she's prettier than me. She's a nine, and I'm just a six on a scale of one to ten."

"Fuck that." Now *I'm* pissed.

"Also, she's an A-lister, and I'm just a costume designer."

"You're not *just* anything. Close that out, Olivia."

"How do you live with that shit?" she demands and tosses her phone into her bag. "It's insulting and demeaning."

"First of all, I don't read that shit," I reply. "Ever. I don't pay attention to the press. Also, I never in my life dated Adrienne. She was a co-star of mine more than six years ago. We played the circuit, posed on the red carpet, all of that stuff because we were *co-stars.* But we were never an item."

She just crosses her arms over her chest and looks out the passenger window.

"Liv, listen to me. You can't pay attention to that drivel. It's all lies. They write that shit to entertain their readers, but they don't care about the truth. Because the truth is boring. Not only did I not date her, but she's not better for me. Not at all. *You're* the one I'm with, and you're the only woman I'm interested in."

Because I love you so completely it makes my gut ache.

But I'm not ready to say that out loud quite yet. Not when it's being forced out of me like this. She wouldn't want that.

"You're right. I'm just touchy today," Liv says. "People suck."

"Yeah, they can. Just focus on what's real. On what's true. You're with me, and I'm sure as hell not going anywhere. Anything else that's said doesn't matter because *we* know the truth."

"Okay." She takes my hand and presses it to her cheek. "I'm okay. I'm sorry."

"Don't be. But, Liv, you're going to have to grow a thick skin where this kind of stuff is concerned because it's going to happen more than either of us likes."

She nods once more. "I'll handle it."

I hope she's right.

CHAPTER 14

~OLIVIA~

"*K*nock-knock."

I turn from my computer and stare at Adam, who's standing in the doorway of my office with a wide grin on his handsome face.

"Hey, what are you doing in town?"

"I had appointments and a table read today. Thought I'd swing by and see if I can steal you for lunch."

I glance down at all the work I still need to get through today and then close the laptop and nod. "Yes. Yes, you can. I'm starving, and my eyes need a break."

"Then let's give them one." He waits while I shut things down and grab my purse. "How's it been going around here?"

"Busy," I reply with a grin. "But that's good. It means we all have a job."

"And that means *I* have a job, so I suppose we can't complain."

"Exactly. Where should we go to eat?"

"You're the local," he reminds me. "But that Mexican place we went to last time was fantastic."

"And it's close by. Only a five-minute walk."

"Let's do it, then." We're quiet as we ride down in the elevator, but by the time we hit the sidewalk outside, there's no lull in the conversation. "I saw the photo of you and Vaughn at Christian Wolfe's dinner."

I scrunch up my nose as he opens the restaurant's door for me. The hostess immediately escorts us to a table.

"There weren't supposed to be phones or cameras there," I say after the waitress drops off a basket of chips and some salsa. "It was a private dinner."

"Once in a while, something slips through," Adam says with a nod. "And it sucks when you think you have some privacy. I'm sorry that happened."

I shrug and set my menu aside. "At least, I looked good, I guess. It would suck if I were in sweats with my hair in a bun."

"I think you'd probably look good then, too."

I press my lips together and narrow my eyes at Adam. "Why are you flirting with me?"

He laughs and shakes his head. "Sorry. Friends, right?"

"Yeah, but if that's weird for you—"

"It's not. Vaughn's clearly smitten with you, and I

have no hard feelings. I like him. He's not the jerk the paps make him out to be."

"No, he isn't," I agree, and then the waitress is back to take our orders. "How long have you been an actor, Adam?"

"Oh, geez, I didn't realize math would be involved today. Let's see, I went to NYU for acting and performing arts, so I guess it's been about ten years."

"Do you have famous actors in your family?"

"No. None at all. My parents are from Wisconsin. Dad's a dairy farmer. I don't know where I get my love of acting from, but it's definitely not from them."

I nod and pop a chip into my mouth thoughtfully.

"Why do you ask?"

"Well, I have a famous dad, but he worked really hard to give my siblings and me as normal a childhood as possible. And it pretty much was."

"I didn't even know he *had* kids until I met your dad about five years ago at an awards dinner, and he told me that he did. He's *very* private. It's well known in the community."

"Yeah, and I'm beginning to realize that giving us a normal life was both difficult and a blessing."

"Vaughn didn't have that same kind of life."

"No." I eat another chip. "He didn't. Being photographed everywhere he goes is just normal to him. I don't think he even knows what privacy feels like. And that's just...hard, you know?"

"I think it would be, yes. What's bothering you?"

I shake my head and realize that I shouldn't be voicing this to Adam. I should be talking it over with Vaughn. "Nothing, really. I guess it's just interesting to me how people end up in the spotlight. Some are born into it, and others seek it out."

"Are you having trouble with the paps?"

"No, just fans. It's an adjustment, but everything's fine. Now, let's talk about you. How are *you?*"

"I'm great. I have three more projects lined up after the one we're about to start with your father, so the next two years or so are spoken for. I'm just happy to have work."

"And how are your parents in Wisconsin?"

"It's just my dad now," he says as the waitress delivers our food. "Mom passed away about three years ago from cancer."

"I'm so sorry." I reach over and rest my hand on Adam's arm. "I don't know what I would do without my mom."

"It was a blessing, honestly. She's no longer hurting," he replies softly. "But my dad's great. Still working with the cows, and I hear he has a girlfriend, so he's not lonely."

"No siblings?" The burrito is *delicious.*

"Three, actually," he replies and spoons some sour cream onto his enchilada. "Two brothers and a sister, all living in my hometown. I have a bunch of nieces and nephews, and I go home during the holidays."

"That's where you should have your house," I say,

thinking out loud. "Not that real estate in LA isn't good, but you should spend your off time in Wisconsin with your family."

"I've been thinking about it," he says with a nod. "Especially now that my dad is older. After we wrap on this movie, I thought I'd go spend a couple of weeks there and look around."

"That'll be good."

Our mealtime goes by fast, and before I know it, we're walking back into Williams Productions and my office.

"Keep me posted on how it shapes up in Wisconsin," I say to Adam. "I'm invested now."

"I will," he says with a chuckle. "I'm sure I'll see you around. I'll be in and out for a couple more days."

"Awesome."

Vaughn walks into my office, surprising me, but I'm excited to see him.

"Hi there," I say to him with a big smile. "Do you have table reads today, too?"

"Uh, yeah. I do." He glances to Adam, who smiles and then turns to me. "I'll get out of your hair. I wanted to go say hi to your dad before I leave."

Adam kisses my cheek, and then he walks past Vaughn and out the door.

"This is a nice surprise," I say as I hurry over and hug Vaughn. "How's your day going?"

"It's...interesting."

"I bet table reads *are* interesting." I turn back to my

desk and try to remember what I was doing when Adam arrived. "I've never sat in on one, but I've thought about it. It just sounds fun."

"Uh, Liv?"

"Yeah." I smile over at Vaughn, but it leaves my lips as I see the angry look on his face. "What's wrong?"

"What was that?" He points to the doorway.

"What was what? Adam?"

"Yeah. What did I walk in on?"

"We just got back from lunch. He popped by and asked me out to lunch, and I went with him."

"And he knows who your dad is?"

"Well, yeah." I blink and frown. "I told him."

"When? When did you tell him?"

I think back and remember, and then my stomach starts to feel funny. "It doesn't really matter."

"I think it does."

I shake my head, but Vaughn walks to me and takes my hand in his. His voice isn't angry when he says, "It matters, Liv."

"Okay." I take a deep breath. "The night you made me mad, and I didn't come to your house like we'd planned. I went out to dinner with Adam, and I let it slip that night."

Vaughn rears back as if I'd slapped him.

"I'm sorry, I completely misjudged this situation," he says as he drops my hand and backs away. "I thought we were exclusive."

"We *are*. Vaughn, I told Adam we're just friends, and he knows that you and I are a...*thing*."

"When was the last time you fucked him?"

Okay, that pisses me off.

"Jesus, Vaughn. I've *never* fucked him. I haven't been with anyone but you since the minute you first walked into my office, and I don't want anyone else. Adam is a friend. He invited me to lunch, that's it. He's nice."

"He put his mouth on you," Vaughn says, his voice hard, and his green eyes full of hurt.

"He kissed my cheek."

"He put his mouth on you," he repeats. "And that doesn't fly with me, Olivia."

"Okay." I nod slowly. "I get it. If the roles were reversed, I'd be pissed off. But I'm not lying when I say that *nothing* happened. He's just a nice man who bought me lunch today. He's nice to me. But I do *not* have feelings for him beyond that. There's no chemistry. There's no fire. For God's sake, I've only seen him in person *twice*. You are the one I care about."

Vaughn rubs his hand over his lips and nods. "Okay."

"You believe me?"

"I do. I believe you. But I still don't like it, and I don't want to ever have a repeat of the way I felt when I walked in here just now."

"I'm sorry," I reply. "It was so innocent, it didn't even occur to me. And I can honestly say that I'll be more considerate in the future. If you would be uncomfortable if you're *here*, I won't put myself in a position you'd not like when you're not here."

"I'd appreciate that," he says, and his voice is softer now. I *think* the storm has passed. But he still doesn't come back to me or pull me against him, and I hate that. "Are we on for dinner tonight?"

"Absolutely."

"Good. Jamal also invited us to go to a party the team is hosting downtown. There will be a band. It sounds fun, if you're up for it."

"Sounds great. I'll swing by my house and grab some clothes for it on my way to your place."

"That's out of the way," he replies with a frown. "Why don't I just meet you there, we'll eat at your place, and then head to the party from there?"

"That works, too."

"Okay, I'll see you later."

"Vaughn." I hurry over to him before he can leave my office. I wrap my arms around his shoulders and kiss him, long and deep. When I pull back, I frame his face in my hands. "I'm really sorry that I hurt you."

"I'm okay," he says and tips his forehead against mine. "Just gave me a bad few minutes, that's all. Adam's a nice guy, but I don't want him dating you."

I smile and squeeze Vaughn close. "He's just a friend. A casual one, at that. I'm all yours."

He kisses my forehead and then pulls away. "I'll see you in a little while."

And then he's gone, and I feel awful.

If it had been the other way around, I might have ripped a bitch's hair out of her head as I pulled her off Vaughn.

I sit behind my desk and start making plans to make it up to him.

∽

VAUGHN'S CAR is already at my house when I pull up, which doesn't surprise me because I'm about fifteen minutes later than I thought I'd be.

But, hopefully, he'll forgive my tardiness.

I walk into the house and find Vaughn chatting with Erin in the living room.

"Sorry I'm late," I announce as I walk in, holding the flowers I bought for him. "But I had to swing by and get these for you."

Vaughn's eyebrow wings up. "For *me?*"

"Yes." I pass him the pink and red roses with a smile. "If I learned nothing else from my father, it's that when you've fucked up, you buy flowers. I hope you like roses."

"I don't think anyone has ever given me flowers before," he says with a half smile. "Thanks. Erin, if you'll excuse us?"

"Sure," Erin says with a knowing smile. "I think I'll go...somewhere."

I laugh as Vaughn slings me over his shoulder and

smacks my ass, then hauls me—and the flowers—up the stairs to my bedroom.

I wave at Erin as he climbs, and then I laugh some more when he tosses me onto the bed.

"I guess this means you forgive me?" I ask as Vaughn very carefully chooses a flower from the bouquet before gently setting the rest on my vanity.

"After I had time to think about it," he says softly, staring down at the pink rose, "I realized that you hadn't done anything wrong. It just looked *really* bad at the time."

I cringe. "Yeah, I'm sorry about that."

Vaughn sets the rose on the pillow next to me and gets to work taking my clothes off. He's always so *thorough* when he undresses me, which only intensifies the lust. The air practically hums with electricity by the time he lowers my panties down my legs and then throws them over his shoulder.

"You undo me," he says softly and reaches for the rose. "You're so fucking beautiful it steals my breath every damn time. And the pink on this rose matches your nipples and pussy perfectly."

"Oh, that wasn't on purpose."

He grins as he drags the bloom down my chest and over my breasts.

"I know. What a fun coincidence." The rose journeys down my stomach, over my belly button, and lower still to my pubis. "Spread your legs, baby."

I couldn't say no if I wanted to. And I definitely don't want to.

I part my legs and sigh when he pulls those petals over my lips, up over my clit, and then replaces the flower with his mouth. My hips buck up off the bed.

He's merciless in how his mouth moves over me, and when his fingers join the party, I cry out.

"Oh, my God!"

"Go over," he commands as his fingers work some kind of magic, and I do exactly as he asks. I fall over the waterfall of overwhelming need and into a pool of satisfaction so deep, I feel as though I might drown.

"Mine," he says as he hurries to push his jeans down his hips, and then he's thrusting into me, hard and fast. "*Mine*, Olivia."

"Yours," I agree breathlessly, overcome with need and love for this man that I feel as though I hardly know—and yet almost as if I've known him forever. It's as though he's a part of me now, and I can't imagine living my life without him in it.

He pushes me over one more crest and follows, growling my name as he comes.

"Holy hell," I whisper, catching my breath. "That was fun. I should buy flowers more often."

Vaughn chuckles and pushes up so he can smile down at me. "That might have been the best make-up sex in the history of make-up sex."

"I agree. And now, I'm *really* hungry."

"Me, too." But he doesn't pull away. He brushes his

hands through my hair and kisses me, soft and slow, like an old-fashioned love song.

And when he does finally pull away, he drags his hand down my torso from my neck to my stomach.

"Mine," he says once more. "Let's eat."

CHAPTER 15

~VAUGHN~

"*F*or fuck's sake, Liv, why do you want me incarcerated?"

Liv laughs at my reaction to the dress she's wearing —at least, I think that's what it is. It's shimmery silver with long sleeves and a high neckline, but the hem ends just below her ass.

"If you bend over, or if there's a strong breeze, you'll be arrested for indecent exposure."

She fastens her earrings and watches me in the mirror with a satisfied grin on her plump lips, which she happens to have painted red.

Not pink.

Red. Bold red.

"I'll be fine," she says. "And don't worry, my boots cover most of my legs."

My mouth goes dry when she steps into boots that

match her dress perfectly and zips them all the way to about three inches above her knees.

Maybe six inches of skin show from the boots to the dress.

It's the most alluring damn getup I've ever seen in my life.

"Did you make this?"

"Of course." She checks herself one more time in the mirror. "You said this was a club party, so I wanted something flirty."

"You achieved it," I reply and walk up behind her, brushing her hair aside so I can kiss her neck. "Just don't bend over."

"I have no plans to. If I drop something, you can fetch it for me."

"Gladly."

I'm just in slacks and a button-down, but with Liv on my arm, I look *damn* good.

The drive into downtown is slow, thanks to a wreck on the freeway, but we finally arrive at the popular club in the heart of Seattle. The team rented it out for the night for a private party, and from the look of things from the outside, it's well-attended.

The bouncer checks my name on the list, and then we're inside. The band plays a cover of an old Maroon 5 song, and tables are full of drinks and food.

Kelly waves us over to theirs. When we arrive, she immediately pulls Liv in for a hug.

"Holy shit, girl, you are *hot.* Where did you get that dress? I need one."

"I made it," Liv says with a smile. "But I could make you one and tailor it to you, make some adjustments to show off all your assets, that sort of thing."

"Take her up on it," I advise Kelly. "One day, her dresses are going to be worth a *lot* of money."

"He's biased," Liv says.

"I think he's right," Kelly replies. "I'll take you up on it for sure. Oh, and, Vaughn, don't forget that I need you in LA on Friday by noon for meetings with all your people."

"Meetings?" Liv asks.

"I have quarterly meetings with the financial people, my agent, things like that. Just business stuff. You should come with me."

"To talk to your agent?"

I lean in and kiss her cheek and then speak directly into her ear. "No, just to be with me. We can go shopping or take in a show. Whatever you want."

She smiles. "Okay."

"Okay." I turn to Jamal as Kelly and Liv start talking about designers and shoes and all the places to shop in LA. "How's the vision?"

"Still blurry," he softly says so Kelly can't hear. "Head's not killing me anymore, though, so that's good."

"Are you gonna play this weekend?"

"Nah, the docs are making me take one more week

off to see if the vision clears. It's not career-ending, and I may just end up needing glasses, but damn, it's frustrating."

"Give yourself some time," I say and clap him on the shoulder. "Rest and let your head heal. You took a hell of a hit. It might have taken ten years off my life."

"Yeah, well, I'll be okay."

"Oh, my God. I hate that guy," Liv says, pointing to the band's lead singer.

"Do you know him?" I ask her.

"Yeah. That's Brax Adler, aka the big jerk who broke Josie's heart."

I raise my eyebrows and watch the frontman on stage. "Josie used to date him?"

"A few years ago. They were pretty serious, and then he was *so mean* to her, and she is the nicest person in the world. I guess that's what happens when you fall for a rock star, although my uncle Leo is awesome and would never be an ass to my aunt Samantha."

"I don't think Brax is a star," Kelly chimes in. "He's just a local musician, although I do hear that he's gaining popularity. One of their songs just went out on national radio."

"Good things shouldn't happen to bad people," Liv says with her eyes narrowed as she sips the martini the waitress just brought her. "Although, this *is* one of my favorite songs, even if it's being sung by a jerk. Let's dance, Vaughn."

"I thought you'd never ask."

Liv laughs and takes my hand, leading me out onto the packed dance floor where the crowd swallows us as she presses her sweet little body to mine, moving against me as if she were made for me.

Because she was.

We dance through so many songs, I lose count. Kelly and Jamal join us, and we take breaks to grab something to drink, but my girl wants to *dance.*

And I'm happy to oblige her.

Finally, around one in the morning, Liv sighs and leans into me. "I should go home. I have to work tomorrow."

"Okay, we can do that."

I check in with Jamal and thank him for the invite. Kelly and Liv talk for another fifteen minutes, and then we're headed out the door.

Lightbulbs flash in our faces, and people shout questions.

I didn't realize the paps would be here tonight.

"Vaughn! Vaughn! Is it true you're seeing Olivia exclusively?"

Liv presses her face to my shoulder, and I wrap my arm around her as we hurry down the sidewalk to my car.

"Have you introduced her to your family?"

"Did you meet because of the movie you're working on?"

"Are you engaged?"

"Did you know she's also seeing Adam Carter?"

That last one fills my chest with a little rage, but I ignore them all and get Liv settled in the car, then walk around to the driver's side and speed away from the mob.

"Shit," Liv says on a sigh. "That was intense."

"I should have realized they'd be there," I mutter, irritated with myself for not thinking of it. "Sorry about that."

"Why do they think I'm seeing Adam?"

I shake my head. "I have no idea. And, frankly, I don't care."

"I'm going to find out." She picks up her phone and starts looking around in places I wish she'd just stay out of, and then she gasps. "Holy fucking shit! There are photos of Adam and me having lunch today. Or yesterday, I guess. What the hell?"

"Eyes everywhere," I mutter and sneak a glance at her phone. Liv is touching Adam's arm in the photo.

"Those slimy bastards," Liv mutters. "It says we had a cozy, romantic lunch in a local restaurant. You idiots. It wasn't romantic! I felt bad that his mom died a few years ago. You suck."

She shoves her phone back into her bag.

"You're really letting this get to you."

"I don't like liars," she grumbles.

"You can't let it get to you, Liv. Stop reading that shit. Like we said the other day, you and I know the truth, and that's all that matters."

"Is it?"

I glance her way and feel my chest tighten. "What does that mean?"

"Nothing. I'm just tired and have a headache. And I probably drank too much. I want to flip those assholes off."

"No reaction is the best reaction."

"You're too calm."

"I think you're upset enough for both of us."

She huffs out a breath and watches the city go by as I drive back to her house.

"I had a good time tonight," I say and reach over to take her hand. "We can't let thirty seconds of stupidity ruin that. You can move that sexy body of yours, by the way."

She rolls her head against the seat and sends me a soft smile.

"I have an aunt who used to be a famous ballerina."

"Of course, you do." I laugh and turn down her street. "You have a fascinating family, you know that?"

"Oh, I know. They're pretty cool. Are you coming in to stay the night?"

"Yeah, I'd rather not sleep without you these days."

I want to ask her to move in with me, but I don't know what she'd think of that, and I'm too tired to have the conversation tonight.

"Good, because I prefer to sleep with you, too."

"Good morning."

I crack open one eye and see Liv grinning down at me, a mug of coffee gripped in her hand.

"I brought you caffeine."

"Time is it?" I ask as I sit up and accept the mug, taking a long sip.

"Seven," she replies and leans down to kiss me. "I have an early meeting at work."

"You're dressed and everything," I point out, the sleep slowly clearing from my foggy brain.

"That happens when a person has an early meeting," she says with a grin and kisses me again. Before I can tug her back down with me, her phone rings. "Hello?"

She scowls and stands to pace the room.

"What? How did you get my number? No, I won't comment on that."

She hangs up the phone and stares at me.

"Who was it?" I ask calmly and sip the coffee.

"*Entertainment Weekly*. They wanted a comment on my relationship with you."

"You said exactly the right thing."

"Yes, but how in the hell did they get my *number*?"

I shake my head and shrug a shoulder. "I don't know. They seem to have ways."

"It's a pain in the ass to have to change my phone number. Damn it."

Her phone rings again. She lets it go to voicemail, and her eyes fly to mine.

"I didn't give out your number," I remind her. "It's not my fault."

Except, it kind of is. They wouldn't be hounding her if she weren't with me. Her phone rings again, and she narrows her eyes at it and then presses her lips together.

She's pissed off.

"Why would anyone put up with this crap?" she demands and looks back at me. "It's invasive and disrespectful."

"It'll calm down," I assure her and stand so I can walk to her and take her shoulders in my hands. "This will all blow over and quiet down. You'll change your number, un-list it, and restrict who has it. For colleagues and people you don't know well, just give them an email address to reach you so there's no chance of that person passing your number along to the wrong people."

"That's *ridiculous*," she stresses. "I should be able to give my number to whomever I choose without being worried that fucking *People* magazine or whoever will try to call me. My God, Vaughn, why would anyone want to live this way? Why would they put up with that?"

I feel my frustration building, and I have to step back. I rub my hand over my mouth. "It's not an everyday occurrence," I remind her. "And I would hope that you'd be willing to tolerate this because I'm in love with you, and being with me brings a whole host of things that are uncomfortable and a pain in the ass, but we can deal with it."

Her mouth opens as if she's about to reply, only when my words sink in, she closes it again and just blinks at me.

"I didn't mean to say it like that. Fuck."

But before I can walk to her and try to smooth things over, she receives a text, and her cheeks go white as the blood leaves her face.

"What is it?"

"*Hi, this is Shelly Moran with* TMZ," she begins, reading aloud, *"and I'd like to request a one-on-one interview with you regarding your relationship with Vaughn Barrymore and why you've kept your real name a secret. I'd also like to ask questions about your father, Luke Williams. Please call me at your earliest convenience."*

"Right, like you'd actually call her," I say, scoffing. "Do they think you're stupid? They'll try anything."

"Vaughn, they've connected the dots to my *dad*. I— I've worked damn hard to keep us separate professionally, and you know it. And just like that, they know. And whether I comment or not, they'll start talking about it."

I nod and blow out a breath. "Honestly, that was bound to happen eventually, with or without me. You're making a name for yourself in this business, and they'll start to dig into your family."

"You don't fucking get it," she says, her white face flushing with anger now. It's quite possible that she might throw something at me. "You don't *care*. This is an invasion of my privacy that I didn't ask for just because I'm screwing around with you."

I narrow my eyes, and my heartbeat picks up. "Is that all we're doing, Liv? I just told you that I love you, and you're pissed because you're inconvenienced by *screwing around* with me?"

"You're not the victim here," she says, shaking her head.

"And neither are you." Jesus, no one has ever been able to cut me to the bone the way Olivia Williams can. "Of course, I *care* that this has hurt you. Jesus, I wouldn't want you hurt for anything in the world, but it happened, and now we deal with it. Your father must have a media department. You can have a rep comment for you, and we'll move on with our lives. In the grand scheme of things, this is just a blip, Liv. Shit like this happens."

"To *you*," she stresses. "Not to me. Because my dad worked hard to protect me from it. And now, less than a month of knowing you, all those years of diligence and hard work are just out the goddamn window."

"Okay, now you're being a little dramatic."

Her eyes narrow menacingly, and I know without a doubt that that was exactly the *wrong* thing to say.

"I have to go. I need to get to work."

She shoves her feet into some shoes and grabs her bag, walking to the door.

"You can see yourself out."

"Come back here and talk to me, damn it."

"I don't have anything to say to you right now," she replies over her shoulder as she hurries down the stairs. "Or, if this is better for you: *No fucking comment.*"

And with that, she marches out of the house, and I'm left standing at the top of her stairs, naked as the day I was born.

"Shit," I whisper and return to her bedroom to get dressed. "What a fucking mess."

I need to start doing some research and make some calls. Someone gave her number out.

And they'll pay for it.

CHAPTER 16

~OLIVIA~

J drive away from my house but don't point the car toward work.

I can't go there.

Instead, I dial my dad's number. "Please answer, please answer."

"What's the story, morning glory?" he says, the way he always does when he answers my calls.

"Are you still at home?"

"Yeah, I was just about to head to the office. What's up?"

"Can you stay there for a few?" I take a deep breath. "I need to come to see you and Mom."

"Sure thing. Come on over. Are you okay, baby?"

"I don't know, I just need to talk to you. I'm almost there."

"Okay, I'll have the coffee ready. See you soon."

He hangs up, and I swallow a lump in my throat. I'm

too damn mad, too confused to cry. I need to talk to my parents.

I hurry out of my car after parking in their driveway and rush through the front door.

"We're in the kitchen," Mom calls out.

I find them both in the kitchen, Dad pouring coffee while Mom spreads jam on some toast.

They look at me and then glance at each other.

It's always been as though they speak their own, silent language. It's a little creepy.

"What's up, Livie?" Mom asks.

"Are the other girls here?"

"No, they're out," Dad says and points to a stool. "Take a seat."

"I might as well just get right to it," I say as I accept a mug of coffee and take a sip. My dad always knows the right way to make it. "I need to know why, *exactly why*, you hate Hollywood so much."

"Has something happened?" Mom asks.

"Several somethings," I mutter.

"Why don't we start with what's going on with you?" Dad suggests, "and then we'll go from there."

I look down into my coffee. "It's mostly paparazzi stuff. Photo leaks, lies, hounding. Which sucks, but I can see that it happens. But then this morning, *TMZ* freaking *texted* me, wanting to know about my relationship with Vaughn *and* why I've hidden that I'm your daughter."

I swallow hard again.

"I'm not ashamed of you, you know that."

"I know," Dad says and leans on the counter. "Did you think you'd be able to keep that side of your life hidden forever?"

"No." I sigh and push my hands through my hair. "I just didn't expect to be ambushed with it. And on the heels of being followed by the paps last night, it just pissed me off."

"Did they follow you home?" Dad's voice is hard as stone.

"No, Vaughn and I went to a party hosted by the Seattle football team, and when we came out of the club, they were there and trailed us to his car. But they didn't follow us from there."

"Small miracles," Mom murmurs. "The paps might be the worst part of your dad's world. Of *your* world now. Hell, we met because he thought I was one of them and tried to steal my camera."

"What?" I stare at both of them. "I never heard that story."

"I was walking the beach, minding my own business," Mom says, "taking pictures of the Sound, and this jerk comes storming over and demands that I erase the photos. I didn't even know who he was."

"It was a bad time for me," Dad says softly. "I know what it's like to live Vaughn's life. At one time, I was the hottest young actor in the business, and they *hounded* me. There was never any privacy. My life was ripe to be picked apart every day. I couldn't date. I couldn't even leave my damn house. I felt like I was in prison.

"Finally, I left acting altogether and came back to Seattle for a while. I hated being followed constantly. It gave me anxiety. Really bad anxiety. So, yeah, I saw a woman taking photos and immediately thought she was aiming for me. Gave me a bad moment. But then I realized that she had no interest in me at all, and that's when I knew that I'd met the woman I'd be with forever."

"That's...*sweet?*"

Mom laughs but then sobers again as she bites into her toast. "Your dad went from being in front of the camera to being behind it. That way, he was in the spotlight less."

"I love making movies, second only to your mom and my kids," Dad agrees. "But I couldn't deal with all of the pressure that came from being the star of the film. The production process, directing the movies, is just as interesting to me and brings a little anonymity with it."

"That's not entirely true," I say, shaking my head. "I know who Spielberg is, and he wasn't an actor."

"I'll always be recognizable because of the work I did when I was young," Dad says. "But since I've been married, my home is in Seattle, and I just make the movies, I'm less exciting to the paps. And I like it that way."

"So, that's why you never wanted us to go with you to LA?"

"Yeah. I didn't want that world to touch you. We worked hard to have excellent security and to make sure that you lived normal lives. And for the most part, the press respected that."

"Easy to do when we're so boring," Mom says with a smile. "We're not exactly newsworthy unless your dad has a premiere or wins an award."

"And that's the way I like it," Dad says. "Now, my amazing daughter, you have a decision to make for yourself. At the end of the day, it's up to you to decide if you're going to maintain the level of privacy I've given you or if you're going to let the world in—and to what degree."

"Being with Vaughn will dictate some of that," Mom adds.

"Being with Vaughn is what started all this mess," I admit with a sigh. "And he just says *it happens.* He acts like it's no big thing. I mean, he said he's sorry but that it's just normal for him."

"Because it is," Dad says. "He's dealt with this since birth. Maybe I sheltered you too much, but you've had two very different experiences."

"I like Vaughn," Mom says with a smile. "He reminds me of someone I love more than anything."

Dad looks down at her in surprise. "Who?"

"You, you big goof." Mom bumps his hip with hers. "He's very much like your dad was at his age, and there's so much potential in front of him. In front of both of you. I don't think there's a wrong answer here, Liv."

"I think there could be jealousy issues. And some other things, too," I admit softly. "Why does it have to be so hard?"

"Because if it were easy, you wouldn't want it," Dad says. "It's your choice. And you don't have to make it today or even tomorrow. But now you know the score. I'd rather you found out now than a year from now when you've invested even more of yourself, and it's harder to walk away—if that's what you want to do."

"I love him," I whisper and hang my head in my hands. "But being with him is so hard. And it's just the beginning."

"Oh, my sweet girl." Mom circles her arms around me and kisses my cheek. "It's tough, but so are you. You'll figure out what's right for you. I know you will. And no matter what, you have us."

"Even if you don't want to admit that you're my daughter," Dad says, making me laugh.

I stay for a little longer and finish my coffee, then decide to go.

"I'm not coming into the office today," I say to my dad. "Sorry."

"Take the rest of this week and start fresh on Monday." He kisses my forehead when we reach my car. "I think the most important thing is for you to talk to Vaughn about this. Maybe he hates it all as much as I did."

"But he doesn't hate the acting part," I say. "And I couldn't ask him to leave that any more than he can ask me not to sew."

"Call me if you need me," Dad says after what looks like an internal struggle.

"Okay. I will. Thanks. I'll have to turn my phone off until I can get a new number, so if you need me for an emergency or something, just call Stella. And, Dad?"

"Yeah."

"Thank you for shielding us from that. I haven't had to deal with it for long, and it's pretty horrible."

"There's nothing I wouldn't do to keep you safe. Nothing."

With that, he winks and then shoves his hands into his pockets before walking back in through the open front door.

Likely to make out with my mom before he goes to work.

I drive back home, relieved to see that Vaughn's car is gone when I get there. I have too much to think about to fight with him some more right now.

But rather than go inside, I lock the car and set off on a walk to the waterfront. It'll be busy at this time of the morning with joggers and cyclists, especially since it's not raining today, but that's okay.

I like to spend time by the water. The noise helps me think.

When I think back over the past few weeks with Vaughn, I have to admit that it's been the paps that have caused the most angst. It started the night in LA when someone took that photo at the dinner party and has only grown since then. Other photos were leaked, including the one of me with Adam yesterday.

Vaughn didn't even bat an eye at that. Sure, we'd already talked about what'd happened, but he'd still been jealous when he discovered Adam in my office yesterday.

He has a demanding job that will take him out of Seattle more than he's here, and I have a career at Williams Productions. I *love* my job and don't plan to leave it. So, what's going to happen? He'll be God knows where, all over the damn globe, filming movies while I'm in Seattle working. And then what? I see lies about him—about *us*—in the tabloids, and we constantly have to reassure each other?

That just sounds exhausting.

But then I think about the man himself and how he makes me laugh, how he makes me feel so secure and so...I don't know, *treasured.* Like when he looks at me, I'm all he sees. He told me he loves me, and I didn't say it back.

Not because I don't feel it, but because I'm so scared and frustrated that I don't know what to do.

This morning was just the icing on the cake.

Maybe I'm not strong enough to live Vaughn's lifestyle, no matter how much I love him.

I make my way back to the house and trudge inside. Stella's on the couch, which surprises me.

"Why aren't you at work?" I ask her.

"I didn't want to go today," she says with a shrug. "It's one of those days when you just need some mental-health time, you know?"

"Yeah," I agree with a nod. "I know. Having one myself."

My lower lip wants to wobble, so I bite it, and Stella's eyes narrow. She stands and reaches for my hand.

"You know what? We're gonna go upstairs and just pull the covers over our heads."

She leads me up to her bedroom, and with our clothes still on, we climb into her bed, pull her thick, blue comforter over our heads, and lie there, facing each other. Her gorgeous blue eyes are worried.

"Wanna talk about it?"

I shake my head. "No. I think I'm all talked out."

"Okay." She reaches for my hand again and holds it in hers, linking our fingers. "When you *do* want to, I'm here for you. Just like always. Until forever. You know that, right?"

"Yeah." The tears come, and I can't stop them. "Yeah, I know that."

She pulls me to her and holds me tightly, rubbing her hand over my back in big, comforting circles as I cry into her shoulder.

"I don't know if I can do this," I whisper. "I don't think I can."

"You don't have to do anything right now. Just breathe, babe."

I don't know what I would do without Stella. She's my best friend. And, honestly, a soulmate to me. She's my person.

And being here, safe under the covers with her, gives me the courage to let the tears come, knowing she won't judge me. I don't have to talk or solve anything.

I can just be.

And that's the biggest gift of all.

"Rocky road and peppermint," Erin says as she comes into Stella's room, carrying tubs of ice cream and three spoons. "I don't know what's going on, but ice cream can't hurt."

"You're the best," Stella says, reaching out to help Erin get everything situated on the bed. She pulls the lids off the containers and tosses them right into the garbage.

There won't be any leftovers.

We've been here in her room all day. We napped after my crying jag, and then we watched old Sandra Bullock movies until Erin came home, found us, and left again for these supplies.

It's the best when your people know you so well that they know exactly what you need without any words being said.

"Do we have to kill someone?" Erin asks as she takes a bite of the rocky road. "I'm pretty sure we can make some calls. Aren't there cousins with ties to the mafia?"

"There are," Stella says, her eyes wide and full of interest. "Oh, my God, Liv. We could call Carmine."

"Nah. No one has to die." I take a bite of peppermint. "You know, when you think about it, we have a really, *really* weird family."

"But it's the best one," Erin declares. "Who cares if it's weird? Why are you sad?"

"I don't know. I have to get a new phone number. The press found mine and started hounding me this morning."

"Okay, that's way annoying," Erin says, rolling her eyes. "I remember hearing that Aunt Samantha had to do that a couple of times."

"Really?" I pull the spoon out of my mouth and stare at Erin. Sam is my dad's sister and is married to Leo Nash—the hottest rock star ever to live. "I never heard that."

"Yeah, I remember my mom talking about it. Said that Sam was pissed because she had to change it for the third time in a year or something. But, you know, everyone loves Leo whether they're, like, really old or our age. So, I guess that's to be expected."

I dip my spoon into the rocky road. "Did *your* mom or dad have to do that? I mean, Will is super famous, too. I would think that Meg probably had to deal with that."

"She lays low," Erin says. "She does the nursing thing and raised us. Mostly, Dad had to deal with the groupies on the road and outside the stadiums. But he's good-natured about it, and Mom always knew that he was coming home to *her*."

I nod, thinking it over. We have quite a few celebrities in our family, whether by blood or marriage or friendship.

"Fame isn't something I've ever given much thought to," I say slowly. "Mostly, because I don't care if *I'm* famous, and we're around celebrities all the time, but they're just normal people, you know?"

"Yeah, but the whole world doesn't feel that way," Stella says. "People get weird about celebrities. Have you ever seen the press from ComiCon? It's *ridiculous*."

"They ask my dad to go every year," I say, shaking my head. "And he always refuses. I bet that pisses his fans off."

"Probably back in the day," Erin agrees. "Especially when those vampire movies came out, and he was a megastar heartthrob."

I wrinkle my nose. "He's my *dad*."

"He's not everyone's dad," Erin reminds me with a smile. "Anyway, is that what this is all about? Being famous?"

"No, it's about deciding if I can be with a guy who's uber-famous and everything that comes with it."

"I don't know if I'd want to do that," Erin says thoughtfully. "But I'm not in love with someone who is, either. I guess my outlook might change if I were and if someone were pulling my hair the way he does yours."

I laugh and have to high-five her.

"You should go talk to Sam," Stella suggests. "It sounds like she's taken the brunt of celeb-wife life. Go ask her about it."

"That's not a bad idea," I reply thoughtfully. "I'll call her tomorrow. If I can get my number replaced. And if I feel like getting out of bed. I was supposed to go to LA with Vaughn tomorrow, but I'm not going. I need a little time away from him to think."

"We just ate a whole gallon of ice cream between the three of us," Erin says and flops back on the bed. "We might be comatose for days."

"I have no regrets," Stella says as she licks her spoon clean.

"Me, neither," I agree. "Maybe later, we'll order pizza for dessert."

"God, I love living here," Erin says with a smile. "There's nothing better than this."

CHAPTER 17

~VAUGHN~

I haven't seen her in more than twenty-four hours, and it's starting to make me twitchy. Jesus, she's like a drug, and I'm having serious withdrawals.

But I figured when I couldn't reach her yesterday that she'd turned her phone off to stop the annoying press calls and that maybe she needed a little time to herself. She was angry yesterday, and so was I.

But I plan to make it all up to her. We're headed to LA today, and we're going to have a good time with some shopping, good food, and just being together.

I jog up the steps to her front door and press the doorbell. When Stella answers, I smile at her.

"Hey, I'm here for Liv. Is she ready?"

"She's not going, Vaughn."

I frown. "What? Of course, she is."

"She's not feeling great," Stella says, and I know it's

229

a lie. "I think she caught a sniffle or something and is sleeping it off upstairs."

"Out of my way."

"Seriously, you should just let her sleep," Stella says, but I ignore her and climb the steps, taking two at a time before opening the bedroom door.

Liv's not sleeping. She's in sweats and a T-shirt and curled up in her chair with a book.

"What's up, Liv?"

"Oh, hey. Um." She swallows, pressing her lips together. "I think I'm going to sit this one out. I don't feel fantastic, and if I'm getting sick, I don't want to pass it on to you."

"You're not sick." I sit on the side of her bed and fold my hands between my knees so I don't reach out and yank her to me to tumble us both onto the bed. "We don't lie to each other, Liv. What's going on? I know you were mad yesterday, but we can talk about it."

"And we will," she says slowly. "We'll talk about it. But you have to get to LA for appointments, and I'm just not up to it right now."

She has dark circles under her eyes as if she's been crying or had a hard time sleeping.

I watch her, willing her to show me some kind of emotion, but her face doesn't change. She looks cold, and that scares me the most.

"Why does it feel like this is the beginning of you breaking up with me?"

She sighs and rubs her fingertips over her forehead. "I haven't decided if that's what I'm doing."

My head comes back as if she's just slapped me.

"Wow."

"We don't lie," she says, echoing my earlier words. "I just need a little time, Vaughn. Just one day, even."

She does cross to me then and cups my face in her hands. I turn and press a kiss to her palm.

"Liv," I whisper.

"I don't know what to do," she says, also in a whisper, and then she's hugging me so tight, it feels desperate.

It feels like goodbye.

"Don't do this, baby."

"Just a little time," she repeats and pulls back. "We'll talk when you come back, okay? Have a super-safe trip and take care of what you need to. I'll see you when you get back to Seattle."

Her green eyes plead with me not to make it harder than it clearly already is, but every cell in my body screams at me to stay. To make her talk to me, to make her understand how much I love her.

"Okay," I say with a nod. "You take your time to think, and I'll be back. That's all I can do, right?"

She doesn't say anything as I turn and walk away, moving down the stairs and past Stella, who's waiting by the door.

"Take care of her," I say to her.

"I am," she says.

231

"If you—or she—needs anything at all, you can call me, day or night. I'll be gone less than twenty-four hours and then I'll be back here. And you won't keep me from her."

"No, I won't." Stella has tears in her blue eyes, which surprises me. She's always struck me as the tougher one. "She's worth all of this, you know."

"She's everything," I reply and walk out while my feet will still carry me away.

~

"I WANT NAMES."

The CEO of *TMZ* just stares at me with arrogant humor. "Not going to happen."

"Listen, I get it, okay? I'm newsworthy. So write or report or whatever all you want about me. But Olivia didn't sign up for that, and having one of your reporters contact her on her private line to inquire about her private life is absolutely unacceptable, and you know it."

"A line was crossed there," he acknowledges. "But you know this business as well as I do, Vaughn. We just sit on different sides of it. You having a new girlfriend is news, no matter who she is. Then, we find out that she's Luke Williams's daughter? That's bigger news. My people will dig. That's just how it goes."

"What'll it take for you to leave her alone?" I ask and

shake my head when Stan scoffs at me. "Really. I want to know. It's an honest question."

"Well, it would take her *not* being with you. Or you not being Vaughn Barrymore anymore. But she's in the business, even if it's only in the background. Her father is Luke Williams, and she's beautiful. Now that the door's been opened, I don't see it closing again."

I nod thoughtfully. "I see."

"I know you do. Of course, if you want to give us an exclusive—"

"No." I stand and march out of his office, moving past his admin and through the bullpen where plenty of reporters take the time to snap my picture and call out questions.

I ignore them all.

When I'm outside, I hail a cab to take me across town to the hotel where I'm meeting with my agent and manager.

Mattias lives in New York and comes to LA twice a year to meet with me in person. He's staying at the Chateau Marmont as he always does when he's in town.

I walk up to the young woman behind the reception desk. Her eyes register recognition, but her smile is nothing but polite and professional.

"How can I help you?"

"I'm here to see Mattias Sunderland."

"Of course," she says and taps on her keyboard, then picks up the phone and calls up to his room. "Mr.

Sunderland, I have Mr. Barrymore here to see you. Of course."

She hangs up and smiles at me.

"I didn't give you my name."

"No need. I'm a fan. You can take those elevators, and you've been cleared up to the thirty-first floor. He's in thirty-one-oh-eight."

"Thanks."

"My pleasure." She smiles again, and I walk away and ride the elevator to Mattias's floor. When I reach his room, the door's already open for me.

"Come on in," he calls out from the bedroom. "I just wrapped up a teleconference meeting with someone in Miami."

He hurries in as I close the door behind me and then pulls me in for a hug.

Mattias has been with me since I was fifteen. I like him, and I *trust* him, which is a big deal for me.

"You look good," he says and gestures for me to sit on the sofa in the sitting room.

"Have you seen the media reports lately?" I ask him.

"I told you to ignore that shit," he reminds me but then nods. "Yes, I have. How is Olivia?"

"Mad as hell."

I stand and pace to the windows to look out over LA.

"I think I'm about to make some big changes in my life, Mattias."

"What, exactly, does that mean?"

I turn back to him, knowing that he won't like what I'm about to say.

"Once I finish the films I'm currently under contract to do, I'm leaving LA. Permanently. No more projects."

His eyes might bug out of his face.

"No. Absolutely, not. You're not going to give up everything you've worked so hard for, over a piece of ass—I don't care how pretty it is."

"Watch it."

His nostrils flare, and my eyes narrow.

"I've made you a *lot* of money, Mattias. Hell, I've made us both a ton of money. I don't need to make more. I can live the rest of my life off the royalties of what I've already done. My grandchildren's grandchildren will never have to worry about money. I'm ready to live a life that makes me happy, not just wealthy."

At that, Mattias deflates and leans back in his chair.

"I meet with the money guys later," I continue. "I'm going to officially buy the Seattle house from my parents. I am *not* going to beg them to just give it to me. I can afford it. And I'm going to sell the Malibu house."

"You'll come out ahead on the real estate," Mattias mutters. "Vaughn, are you sure? You love to act."

"Do I?" I tilt my head to the side and then walk over to sit on the couch again. "I don't know. I'm good at it. I know that. But I was born into it. I didn't have to move here from the Midwest and wait tables or be a stripper while taking acting lessons and trying to get my foot in the door. I was privileged to have my parents' contacts, and I had every leg up there is in this business."

"That doesn't make you less worthy of your status and position."

"No, it doesn't. I've worked hard, and we both know it. I like my job. I enjoy the work. But I *love* her. And the garbage that comes along with my life has hurt her, Mattias. I won't have that. I already spoke with Stan at *TMZ* today—"

"*Alone?*"

"Yeah. Because I'm pissed, and he confirmed what I already knew. If I want to lead any kind of a normal life, I need to back away from the spotlight, not walk right into it. So, we're going to try that for a while. It may not be forever, but I can afford some time off."

"Hollywood may not want you back in a couple of years, Vaughn. You're hot *now*. If you break that momentum, you may not get it back."

"That's okay." I'm surprised to realize that I truly mean what I'm telling him. I believe it down to my soul. If I never acted again, I could live with that.

But I know I'm not okay with the idea of living without Olivia.

"Okay," he says at last. "I won't pursue anything else for you until or unless you give me the go-ahead."

"Great."

"What about special appearances, awards shows, things like that?"

"I'll do little things here and there," I concede. "And

I know the next couple of years will be busy. That documentary about my family is about to come out, and I'll have to do press for that."

"And you have four films lined up," he reminds me.

"I'll keep those commitments," I assure him. "And then, we'll slow it down."

"Is she worth it?"

"Oh, yeah, she is."

He nods and stands when I do, shaking my hand.

"I'd better be invited to the wedding."

I laugh but don't deny that that's my plan. "Front row," I assure him. "I'm ready to have a little fun."

"Okay. When is your next meeting?"

I check my watch. "In an hour. Downstairs. Since I was here, the money guys are coming to me."

"Good. We can have a late lunch."

"Sounds good to me."

"You can have the house," my dad says on the phone. We're in the middle of the financial meeting, and my financial advisor insisted that I call my dad right then and there. "I don't use it, and your mother hasn't been there in a decade. You should have it, Vaughn."

"I'm happy to buy it from you," I reply, reiterating what I already said. "It doesn't bother me."

He's quiet for a moment, and I look up into my advisor's face.

Joe narrows his eyes.

I knew Dad would make me buy it.

"No," he says at last. "I'll have the deed transferred to your name in the morning. It's yours."

"If you're sure, thank you. I appreciate it."

"You're welcome."

And then he hangs up, and Joe sighs.

"Well, he's still not warm and fuzzy, but he might be getting softer in his old age," I say as I set the phone aside. "I guess that's a couple million that we don't have to worry about."

"When do you plan to sell the house here?" Joe asks, making some notes.

"As soon as possible," I reply. "When I need to be in LA, I can get a hotel. Seattle is home."

"Okay, we can get you set up with a real estate agent tomorrow morning, if that works."

I frown. I was supposed to be back in Seattle by tomorrow morning, but I can extend it by a few hours. The end result will be worth it.

"I can manage that," I confirm and make a mental note to get a message to Liv. "It's ready to be shown anyway. I'm barely there. What do you think fair market value is?"

"In Malibu?" Joe asks and then laughs. "Ten million. Easy. We'll see what the realtor says tomorrow. Do you want me to be there for that meeting?"

"Yes, if you can manage it."

"No problem. On a personal note, I want to say that I'm proud of you, Vaughn."

I look up in surprise.

"I think it's time you chase some happiness." Joe winks and then slides his glasses back up on his nose. "Now, let's talk about the trust fund."

It's more than an hour later when I walk out of the hotel. A woman walks down the steps ahead of me, but she slips and falls right on her butt.

"Hey, I've got you," I say as I help her to her feet. She's in heels and a fancy pink dress.

And she's completely drunk.

"Oh, thanks," she slurs and points down to the curb. "That's my cab."

I wrap my arm around her waist and help her down to the waiting car. When I open the door, I look at the driver.

"Do you know where she's going?"

"Yeah, I have the address," he confirms.

"Thanks, handsome," the woman says with a grin and plants a kiss on my cheek. "You know, you look like Vaughn Barrymore."

"I get that a lot." I help her into the car, and she waves as it pulls away.

I need to get back to the house and get ready for the realtor tomorrow.

The sooner I can get home to Liv and make things right, the better.

CHAPTER 18

~OLIVIA~

*I*t's amazing how time really can make you feel better. I woke up this morning feeling refreshed and yanked out of my funk. I took a shower and pulled myself together, even applied some lipstick to give myself just a little extra kick, and then set off to get my day going.

My first order of business was a new phone number. Every time I turned my old one on, I had more messages and missed calls from the press.

That didn't help matters.

I also couldn't check in with Vaughn to make sure he got to LA safely or to find out when he was coming back to Seattle. I never realized how attached to my phone I really was.

Vaughn did send a message through Stella that he wouldn't be back until this afternoon, which was nice of him.

I haven't been able to shake off the look on his face from yesterday when I admitted that I didn't know if we were breaking up or not. He'd looked...devastated.

He'd looked the way I felt.

I pull up to the cell phone store and prepare myself for at least an hour spent with them, but I'm surprised when I walk back out only thirty minutes later with not only a new number but also a new phone, with all my stuff already transferred over.

"Technology is getting a little easier," I mutter when I sit in the driver's seat of my car and send a group text to the family.

We have a group text set up with all of the aunts, uncles, cousins, and grandparents for emergencies.

I bite my lip and stare out the windshield for half a second.

This isn't technically an emergency.

But it'll take me an hour to send a text to everyone individually.

"Group it is," I mutter as I tap out the message.

Me: HEY, GANG. THIS IS OLIVIA. NOT AN EMERGENCY. JUST WANTED TO LET YOU KNOW THIS IS MY NEW PHONE NUMBER. PLEASE DELETE THE OLD ONE. NO NEED TO REPLY.

I hit send and then immediately send another message, this time just to Vaughn.

Me: HEY, IT'S LIV. NEW NUMBER ALERT. I HOPE ALL IS WELL DOWN THERE.

With that done, I set off but don't go home. I head

north on the freeway, out of Seattle, and take an exit about ten miles out of the city. I make my way to the cliffs and park in front of the house I know almost as well as I do my parents' home.

I knock and grin when my uncle Leo answers the door. He smiles and immediately folds me into his arms in a big hug.

"Well, hey there, ladybug. This is a treat."

"I didn't know if you'd be home." I look to my left and see Aunt Samantha walking into the foyer. As soon as she sees my face, she gives me a wink.

"Let's go into the library for some girl talk," Sam says and takes my hand.

"I will not be participating in the girl talk," Leo says and kisses Sam's cheek. "Let me know if you need anything, Sunshine."

"Thanks, babe."

Sam leads me into a two-story room, lined floor to ceiling with bookshelves—completely full of books.

"Good God, I could just live in here," I say with a sigh as I sit in the corner of the couch, bringing my feet up under me.

"I spend a lot of time in here," Sam agrees as she faces me, resting her head on her hand. "What's going on with you?"

"Maybe I just wanted to come by for a chat."

She smiles, her eyes so much like my dad's that it surprises me sometimes, and then wrinkles her nose. "We both know that's not true."

"Have my parents talked to you?"

"Not in a few days."

"Do you know I've been dating Vaughn Barrymore?"

"That, I knew. He's a hottie. Good job, toots."

I laugh and already know this was the right move. My aunt Sam is the absolute *best*.

"He *is* pretty hot," I agree. "But it's been interesting over the past few days."

I outline everything that's happened, how Vaughn and I have handled things, and when I'm done, Sam just shakes her head.

"I think you overreacted."

I feel my jaw drop, and she holds up a hand.

"Just hear me out, okay? I know it's hard, and maybe you're just wired too much like your dad. I was there when things got crazy back in the day with the press, fans, and tabloids. They were ruthless. Luke didn't enjoy it at all. I don't think *anyone* enjoys it, but some can tolerate it.

"Luke couldn't. And he adapted and changed his life accordingly. You're like him in so many ways. Maybe this is another one. But I can tell you that this all sounds very normal to me for the celebrity status that Vaughn has."

"I was afraid you were going to say that. And, yeah, I think I might have been a bit too bitchy about it, but I didn't expect it."

"I get that. If I don't have to change my number at

least once a year, Leo and I worry that his popularity is starting to dim."

I smile at her, and she shrugs.

"It sounds silly, but it's sort of true. Women pine after my man. I mean, look at him. He's hot, he's talented, and he's a musician. It's the rock-star thing. Vaughn is a megastar actor, and that's kind of the same thing. He gets attention. So, this is normal, and it's not going to lighten up. And it's probably not going away."

"Right." I sigh again and nod.

"You have to decide if it's something you can live with. Do you trust him?"

"Yes. I trust him. I know he's totally into me. He wouldn't betray me or anything like that."

"Great. Being confident is the number-one thing. Leo only has eyes for me and always has. Because I know that to be true, I can handle everything else."

I should have come to see her sooner. She's totally right and makes it all sound so simple.

"So, trust isn't the issue," she says. "What is?"

Before I can answer her, my new phone pings, and I glance down to find a text from my sister.

"Sorry, this is Chelsea. Better check—" I scowl when I open the message.

Chelsea: IF YOU WANT, I'LL CUT HIS BALLS OFF THE NEXT TIME I SEE HIM.

And under the message is a photo of Vaughn with a woman in a pink dress in front of a cab. She's kissing his cheek, and his arm is around her.

"It's things like this."

I show Sam the message, and she shrugs as if it's no big deal.

"You have no idea what the context of that photo is," she says. "That could be a fan. It could be a friend. It could be his *sister.*"

"He doesn't have a sister," I mumble but know she's right. "And, honestly, I don't care who she is. You're right. She could be anyone. But I have a feeling this kind of thing will be constant, and it's kind of annoying."

"It is if you let it be," she agrees. "Your first step is to ignore all of the noise. It's 99 percent bullshit anyway. Get off social media. Or, if you want to stay because I know you like to get inspiration for your designs, control what you see. Don't seek out the hate and lies. And, if you know you can't do that, grow some thick-as-fuck skin, girl."

"Dad really shielded us from a lot of shit, didn't he?"

"Oh, yeah." She smiles. "And that's okay. He loves you. Think of it like this, you either figure out a way to deal or break it off. Because if you stick it out, and all you do is complain and throw a fit *every single day* because of this kind of garbage, you'll annoy the hell out of each other, and it'll end badly."

"I can see that," I say with a nod. "I guess I can't ask him to become a hermit."

She laughs. "No, but maybe there's some room for compromise in there. You have to talk to Vaughn, not me—an old lady who's married to the hottest man on the planet. Leo and I made it work for us. We've had slips here and there, but we figured it out. If Vaughn's the one for you, you'll figure it out, too."

"You're super-smart," I say.

"I'm your favorite aunt," she says with a satisfied grin. "It's okay, you can admit it."

"You're my favorite aunt named Sam," I say with a laugh, and she narrows her eyes at me.

"How dare you? I give you the best advice of your life, and this is the thanks I get?"

We're giggling as Sam walks me to the door.

"You'll be great, baby girl. Oh, by the way, I'm going to need a new dress for a fancy thing that Leo has to go to in a couple of months."

"What kind of fancy thing?" I ask her.

"The Grammys," she replies with a shrug, and I stare at her.

"Holy shit, Sam! That's *huge.*"

She nods. "I know. He's up for best songwriter. It's pretty fucking awesome."

"We'll come up with the best dress that's ever been on your body. I promise."

"I can't wait."

I hug her and then walk back out to my car, feeling as if a huge weight has been lifted.

I was acting like a complete jerk over something that Vaughn had no control over.

And I owe him an apology.

I haven't heard back from him, but he could be in the air, so I just drive home. When I pull into the driveway, I'm surprised to see Vaughn there, sitting on the front steps.

He looks tired and worried. And I feel awful that I made him feel that way.

I get out of my car and offer him a small smile.

"Why didn't you go inside?"

He shrugs a shoulder. "I didn't think I deserved to."

I raise a brow. "Okay, so I'm not the only dramatic one."

That makes him laugh a little, and my shoulders loosen as I sit next to him on the steps and lean against him.

"I'm glad you got back safely. We have some stuff to talk about."

"You don't know the half of it," he says and looks down at me. His mouth is just mere inches from mine, and I want to kiss him.

But I wait.

"I'm not letting you break up with me, not over the fucking press, Liv. I love you too much."

"I love you, too."

His mouth closes, and he swallows.

"Okay."

"I'm sorry," I add. "I handled things really poorly. · Okay, I was a horrible human being, especially given that it's not your fault. I *know* it's not your fault. You're excellent at your job, and that means that you get a lot of attention."

His shoulders droop as if he's been holding the weight of the world on them and it's suddenly been lifted.

"I'm sorry, too," he says. "I should have taken your concerns more seriously. It's just such a normal part of my life. It doesn't feel big anymore. But it's not normal for you."

"No, it's not. Not at all. It might take me some time, but we'll figure it out."

He shakes his head, and now it's my turn to be nervous, but it doesn't last long.

"I tried to find out who leaked your number, but so far, no one's spilling their guts on that."

"It doesn't matter," I assure him. "Really, it doesn't."

Vaughn licks his lips and keeps talking. "I'm going to back off on stuff once I finish up with some projects and complete some commitments."

"What does that mean?"

His green eyes meet mine, and he smiles softly.

"I'm going to follow your dad's example for a while. Maybe not to the extreme he does, but I'm not going to act in movies much moving forward."

"Vaughn, I can't ask you to do that—"

"You didn't," he replies. "I'm selling the Malibu house; it went on the market this morning. And the Seattle house is mine now. Your job is here, and I want to be where you are, Liv."

My eyes fill with tears, but I don't care. "I don't want you to leave acting, Vaughn. Base out of Seattle? Yes, that's awesome, and I'm thrilled that you want to do that. But you absolutely will *not* leave acting altogether just for me."

"I'm doing what's best for *us.* I've done what's expected of me for a long-ass time, you know? And I like the work. It's not that I don't. But I *love* you. You're the most important piece of my life, and if you're unhappy or insecure, I need to do whatever I can to take care of you. That's how this works. Jesus, I've never loved anyone the way I do you, and I'm not going to lose you over something that's so easily fixable."

"Leaving your career isn't going to fix this," I reply and cup his cheek in my hand. "I truly believe we can make this all work, Vaughn. We can *really* fix it, not just put a bandage on it. Maybe we can talk to my parents and ask them for some tips. I know you enjoy your job, and damn it, you've worked hard to get where you are. I don't want you to stop acting any more than you'd want me to stop sewing."

He frowns and takes my hand in his, linking our fingers. "I just want to do the right thing for you."

"And I love you for it. We need to do what's right for both of us. Compromise. It's not all about me. Yeah, the paparazzi threw me for a loop, but I'm a strong woman. I'll figure it out. Hell, Chelsea sent me a photo of you with some woman in a pink dress, and I totally blew it off. See? I'm doing better already."

His brows draw together in a frown. "What woman in a pink dress?"

I laugh and climb onto his lap, straddling him on the porch for the world to see, and wrap my arms around him, kissing him for all I'm worth.

His arms encircle me, and he holds me tightly as he kisses me back. His hand drifts up my back to my hair, and he grips it, making me smile.

"Can we start over?" he asks, tipping his forehead to mine. "I would like to take my girlfriend on a date."

"We don't have to start over," I whisper. "Nothing's broken. We just hit a speed bump, that's all. And, yes, I would love a date."

"Great." He stands with me in his arms and sets me on my feet, then frames my face in his hands and kisses me hard. "I have to go, but I'll be back at six to pick you up."

"How should I dress?" I ask as he walks down to his car.

"Nice," he says. "Think fancy."

I raise a brow. "Ooh la la."

Vaughn laughs as he gets into his car, waves at me, and then drives away.

"WHERE ARE you going dressed like that?" Stella asks from my bedroom doorway, holding a mug of tea. "Did I miss something?"

"Vaughn's picking me up soon for a date. He said to think fancy."

"Well, you definitely did that," Stella says as she takes in my long, teal, slip of a dress with its spaghetti straps. It's velvet and feels amazing on my naked skin.

There's no room in here for underwear.

"So, I take it things are better?"

I finish primping and then turn to my bestie and nod. "Yeah. Things are better. I'll tell you all about it later."

"Well, I'm jealous that you get to dress up and go somewhere fancy tonight," she says with a smile. "I want to hear all about it later for sure. Have fun. Make good choices."

I laugh and kiss her on the cheek, then rub the lipstick off her skin.

"Yes, ma'am. Don't wait up."

"I suspect I'd be up for a couple of days if I did," she says, just as the doorbell rings. "There's your prince charming. You wait here. I'll answer the door so you can make a grand entrance."

Before I can answer, Stella hurries down the stairs, and I hear her open the door.

"Wow, you clean up nice," she says, and I grin. I wonder what he's wearing. "Liv, your date's here!"

I come out of the bedroom and make my way down the stairs.

Vaughn's mouth gapes.

The red roses in his hand fall to his side when his hand drops.

I've never felt sexier in all my life when his eyes travel up and down my body with lust shining in them.

"Hi," I say as I approach, taking in his black tux and the red rose on his lapel. God, he's just beautiful. There's no other word for him. "Are those flowers for me?"

"Huh? Oh, yeah." He holds the bouquet back up. "These are for you. I have more for you, but you have to come with me to get it."

"Gladly." I bury my nose in the flowers and breathe deeply. "These smell so good."

"I'll put them in water for you," Stella offers, taking the roses from me. "Have fun, kids."

She winks and walks toward the kitchen.

"Shall we?" Vaughn asks, holding out his arm for me to take.

"We shall," I confirm, and with my small clutch in one hand, I take his arm with the other, and we walk out to his car. "Where are we going?" I ask once we're settled in and driving away from the house.

"To my place," he says.

"We got dressed up to stay *in*?"

Vaughn laughs and pulls my hand up to his lips, nibbling on my knuckles. "You'll see. I have a plan."

I lean my head back and look over at him. Light dances over his face as the sun sets, sinking into the ocean. When he glances my way, his green eyes full of so much promise, I don't think I could be in love any more than I am at this moment.

"What are you thinking?" he asks.

"That you're hot."

He laughs and shakes his head, then pulls into his long driveway. When we reach his house at the top of the hill, he puts the vehicle in park and turns to me.

"Stay put. I'll open your door for you."

"All right."

He hurries around the hood of the car, opens my door, and holds out his hand for me.

"Welcome to my home," he says and kisses my hand.

"Thank you."

I can't stop smiling.

When he leads me inside the house, and I see all the candles and hear the soft music playing through the surround sound, I get a little gooey.

"This is pretty romantic."

"You haven't seen anything yet." He leads me to the dining room, where he has the table set for two with more candles. And when someone walks around the corner from the kitchen, I jump.

"Oh, God." I press my hand to my chest and laugh. "I wasn't expecting that."

"I apologize," the man says. "Dinner is ready when you are, sir."

"Great, give me just five minutes," Vaughn says and holds a chair out for me.

"You had dinner catered?"

"I don't cook," he says with a grin. "I'm good at a lot of things, but not in the kitchen. So, given that I want to keep you alive, yes, I had food brought in."

Vaughn sits across from me and reaches for a red box wrapped with a bow. He passes it to me.

"This is for you."

CHAPTER 19

~VAUGHN~

I don't think I've ever been so nervous in my life. Not when I landed my first leading role. Not when I had to give my first speech.

Never.

Liv's green eyes meet mine, and she smiles. "You didn't have to buy me anything."

She opens the box, and when she pulls out a key, she frowns.

Okay, maybe this was stupid, but I've never asked someone to move in with me before. I don't have any rehearsals under my belt.

"So, the front door doesn't actually take a key," I say as I try to muddle my way through. "It's a code, but this is symbolic. I want you to move in here. With me."

Olivia blinks in surprise and bites her lip.

"Yeah, it's fast. But before I know it, I'll have to be

gone on location again, and I just want to be with you as much as I can. I'm a selfish man, and I want *you*."

"It *is* fast," she agrees softly.

"You can change anything in here that you want. Go crazy. I don't care. I want you to make it yours because I want this to be your home. *Our* home."

"Wow," she whispers.

"Is that a no?"

"It's a wow," she replies and then grins at me. "Yes, I'll move in with you."

I close my eyes in relief, and then I pull her hand to my lips. "Thank God, I was afraid that was about to take a *very* embarrassing turn."

"I was just surprised. You surprise me often."

"I also have this for you," I say and pass another box over the table.

"Do *not* ask me to marry you today," she says, shaking her head. "Because I love you, and I'll move in here, but this is still new and—"

"That's not what it is," I assure her. "Even *I* know when to chill."

She laughs and opens the box, then sighs in that way women do when they see something that sparkles.

"Oh, how pretty." She immediately pulls the diamond earrings out of the box and fastens them to her ears. "These are stunning. But it's not my birthday or anything."

"Presents just because are more fun," I reply and enjoy the way the jewels sparkle on her ears. "Later, I'm going to make love to you, and you'll wear only those earrings."

Her eyes shine with interest. "Deal."

DINNER WAS DELICIOUS. The staff has all left, and now I'm here, alone, with Olivia. Exactly where I want to be.

"This is nice," she murmurs against my chest as we shuffle across the floor, slow dancing to a new Bruno Mars tune. "I needed to work off that pasta."

I grin and kiss the top of her head. "I love this dress. It feels great."

"Velvet is just so *good*," she says with a sigh. "But it's a bitch to work with. Totally worth it, though. Sorry, I geek out over fabric."

"I don't mind. You'll have to pick a room for sewing."

She pulls back and smiles up at me. "A sewing and fitting room would be *awesome*."

"We can do that." I kiss the tip of her nose and let my hand drift down to cup her ass. "It doesn't feel like you're wearing anything under this amazing dress."

The light in her eyes dances. "Because I'm not."

I stop cold, and my dick twitches. "Excuse me?"

"There's no space in here for anything but me."

"That decides it."

I pick her up and, as she giggles in my ear, carry her

up to my bedroom. I could take her on the couch, or in the kitchen, or *anywhere.*

And I will, eventually.

But tonight, I want her in my bed.

When she slides down my body, I gather her dress in my hands and then pull it up and over her head as she raises her arms, helping me.

"Fuck me," I mutter when she's standing gloriously naked before me. "Just that gorgeous strap of velvet was hiding this."

"Clothes are fun," she says with a grin. "And you have *way* more of them on than I did."

My nerves are raw by the time I shed the last piece of clothing, finally out of that monkey suit, and reach for my woman. She fits against me like the missing piece of a puzzle.

And she is.

"I love your skin," I say as I urge her back to the bed. "And I'm going to explore all your nooks and crannies tonight."

That brings a quick grin to her gorgeous face.

"My nooks and crannies look forward to that."

I kiss her, bite her lip, and then lay her back, flipping her over onto her stomach. Her skin is smooth and soft, and I love exploring all the lines and curves of her back, shoulders, and down her spine to her ass. I pepper her with wet kisses and grin when I notice that she has to grip tightly onto the bedding.

"Ah, this nook is awfully alluring." I drag my finger

down the crack of her ass to her slick folds. "So fucking sexy."

"Mm," she moans into the pillow and pushes her ass into the air.

"Like that, do you?" I bite the fleshy part of her ass, kiss over the small of her back and up to her neck, where I grip her thick hair in my fist, just the way she likes it, and tug as I slip inside her.

She jerks around me.

"Holy shit," she breathes. "Just like that."

Jesus, she's just fucking...*everything.* I've never felt this way about anyone, and it's completely over-whelming.

No one's ever been this important.

This damn *vital.*

And she's all mine.

I pull out and flip her over, spreading her wide and plunging right back inside of her. Her hand drifts down, and she rubs circles over her clit, and that's my complete undoing.

"Ah, fuck, babe."

She jerks, contracts, and I can't hold back any longer.

"Wow," she says for the second time of the evening and kisses my shoulder. I'm lying on top of her.

I don't know if I have the strength to roll over.

"I love you," she whispers in my ear.

Suddenly, my strength is revived, and I push up to smile down at her.

I'm still inside her, and I'm swamped with love.

"I love you, too, babe."

God, I love her so much.

And this is only the beginning.

"THAT POOL IS TO *DIE* FOR," Stella says when she and Drew come in from checking it out. "We need to have pool parties next summer."

"Done," I reply with a grin.

"Where do you want this one?" Liam asks, carrying a big box marked *sewing*.

"I have a room for that," Liv says and motions for her cousin to follow her. "Down the hall here."

"Wow. I don't have to climb stairs for once," Liam says sarcastically.

"We brought food," Natalie announces as she and Luke walk in through the open front door. "And I want to check the place out."

"Come on in," I say. "Liv's the foreperson here. I'm about to go out to the truck for more boxes."

"She has a lot of crap," Luke says with a smile and slaps my shoulder in greeting. "And now it's in your house instead of mine."

"Lucky you," Liv says with a laugh as she rushes past me toward the moving truck. "I think I might have forgotten my bobbins."

"I don't know what bobbins are," I admit to Luke,

who only laughs. "And, yes, I'm the lucky one. Want the grand tour?"

"I do," Natalie says. "This is a great place. The view is spectacular. I could take some great shots from up here."

"Come up anytime," I offer and lead the two of them through the house while Liv barks orders to Drew, Stella, and Liam.

"We're going to Iceland for Christmas," Luke says when we're walking down the steps from the second floor.

"Yeah, I heard that you were all going," I reply.

"No," Nat says, shaking her head with a smile on her gorgeous face. "*We're* going. If our girl's living with you, you're one of us. So, you'll be joining us."

I stop on the last step and stare at her for a moment.

It hadn't really occurred to me until right now that they might just include me as a part of their family.

"I can make that work," I say slowly. "Just tell me what you need from me."

"Show up," Luke advises, pats my shoulder again, then walks past me. "I'm gonna go find my daughter."

He walks away, and Natalie watches him go, then pats my arm.

"You're one of us now. You know that, right?"

"I guess I do now."

"In our family, it's an all-or-nothing sort of thing."

"It's a good thing I like all of you."

"Isn't it, though?"

We watch as Luke and Olivia come in, both carrying boxes. He says something that makes her laugh, and then she glances around, looking for me.

When her eyes meet mine, she winks.

My heart stutters.

"Well, look at that," Natalie says with a happy sigh. "That's exactly what I came here to see."

"What's that?" I ask without looking away from my girl.

"That smile. She loves you, you know."

I rub the center of my chest over where I feel a small ache. "Not as much as I love her. Not nearly as much."

EPILOGUE

~OLIVIA~

"*I*t's raining," Vaughn says as if that should mean that I *don't* do yoga this morning.

"It's a good thing I don't plan to do warrior's pose outside," I reply as I unroll my mat. I've started being more mindful of my body and moving it every day in some way during the last month or so since I moved in with Vaughn.

Yoga has been a big part of that.

He's not as impressed with it, but if he's home, he does it with me.

"No phones," I remind him, and he shrugs, taking his out of the room before coming back to join me. I love this sunroom. Even with the rain falling, it's beautiful to see the city covered in gray through the droplets on the glass.

It looks like art.

Over the next thirty minutes, Vaughn and I work

our way through the simple poses called out by the woman on my computer set on a chair in front of us.

When we're finished, sweaty, and all stretched out, we hold our hands as if in prayer over our chests and say, "Namaste."

"Don't you feel ready to tackle the day now?" I ask as I close the laptop. "Kelly and Jamal will be here any second."

"I'm ready to tackle *you*," he says and wraps his arm around my waist. But while he kisses me, I hear the doorbell ring. "That's them. We'll pick this up later."

I laugh and follow Vaughn to the front door, where Kelly and Jamal are waiting with Paisley, who squeals when she sees Vaughn.

"Bon!"

"Hey, gorgeous girl," Vaughn says, kissing her cheek as he pulls her into his arms. "How's my best girl?"

"Iv!" she says, and I blink in surprise, then let out a little gasp.

"Oh my gosh, she knows my name."

"She's saying all kinds of words these days," Kelly says as we all walk toward the kitchen. "I love what you've done in here."

I take a second to glance around, happy with the little feminine touches that I've added here and there. Nothing crazy but just a few things.

"What was wrong with the way it was before?" Vaughn wants to know.

"Nothing, if you're a bachelor," Jamal says with a

wink for me. "I can't believe you're living with this jerk."

"He's only a jerk sometimes," I reply and then giggle when Vaughn scowls at me. "I'm just kidding. You're not a jerk at all."

Vaughn's phone starts to ring, so Kelly takes the baby while he answers.

"Hello?" His eyes meet mine. "You're kidding."

I tilt my head to the side. "Who is it?"

"Wow, that's incredible. Thank you so much. I'm honored."

He hangs up and stares at me.

"What just happened?" I ask.

"Spill it," Kelly says.

"I just got the call that every actor dreams of but few get. I've been nominated for an Academy Award."

I blink as my blood rushes through my body. "Oh my God. OH MY GOD!"

I run to him, leap into his arms, and kiss him so hard.

"Holy shit, this is so great! I'm so proud of you."

"Hell yes, that's what I'm talking about," Jamal says and does the whole manly handshake-hug thing while Kelly and Paisley dance around the kitchen.

Now *my* phone rings. Without glancing at it, I answer.

"Hello?" I kiss Vaughn's cheek.

"Olivia Conner?" a voice says.

"Yes, this is she."

The blood rushes through my head, roars in my ears, but I make out the words. "You've been nominated for an Academy Award for best costume design for your work in *Small Town Girl*."

I blink at Vaughn, who just grins at me. He can obviously hear what's happening.

"Are you sure?" I say at last.

"I'm absolutely sure. Congratulations, Miss Conner."

"Thank—thank you."

The phone slips from my hand, and Vaughn catches it before it crashes to the floor.

"Holy shit."

"Holy shit is right," he says and swings me around in celebration as the other two whoop and holler, and Jamal asks where the champagne is. "You are incredible."

I can only stare at him. "We're *both* nominated."

He grins like a loon. "You're gonna win."

"Vaughn, this is—I don't even know what this is."

"You're gonna *win*." He pulls me to him. "So fucking proud of you, babe."

"I'm proud of us both," I inform him. "We need to celebrate."

"I found the champagne," Kelly announces as she pours four flutes full of the bubbly wine.

Jamal holds his glass up in a toast. "To two of the best, most deserving people I know. Here's to kicking ass and taking names."

"Here's to the freaking *Oscars*," Kelly echoes as we all take a sip.

I smile, feeling all bubbly inside, just like this champagne. "And here's to having everything I never knew I wanted. Here's to love and friendship."

I HOPE you loved The Secret! The next book in the Single in Seattle series, THE SCANDAL, is coming on July 12, 2022. You can get all of the details and preorder right here: www. kristenprobyauthor.com/the-scandal

THE SCANDAL IS AN ALL-NEW **marriage of convenience, age-gap novel from** *New York Times* **bestselling author Kristen Proby, set in her Single in Seattle Series featuring Stella McKenna!**

WHO KNEW that weddings in Vegas were the real deal? I certainly didn't when I agreed to marry my co-worker while on a bender in Sin City. Now, I need a quick annulment, which means I need an attorney, STAT.

Honestly, with a name like Grayson Sterling, Esquire, I expected an old man in a three-piece suit. But the guy behind the desk is anything *but* stuffy and old.

Tall and sexy with tattoos and striking blue eyes, I simply can't take my eyes off him, and I have no intention of declining his offer of a date...and more. So much more!

The conversation between us is good, and the man should win awards for his bedroom escapades. I find myself trusting him in ways I never thought I would—until he breaks that trust.

Gray insists he can fix it.

He claims he loves me.

But I don't know if we can survive this.

WOULD you like a detailed glossary of who's who in this Single in Seattle world? You can visit my site to see it here: www. kristenprobyauthor.com/seattle-family-tree

BONUS EPILOGUE

~LUKE WILLIAMS~

I'm ready to get out of the office and go home to my bride. It should be quiet this evening with no kids around, so I plan to spoil Natalie, make love to her, and just cherish her.

She deserves that and more.

And I have a little extra something in my briefcase for her. I just can't seem to stop buying things for her, even after all our years of marriage.

"Excuse me."

I glance at the doorway and see Vaughn. "Hey there."

"I'm sure you're ready to head out, but can I have a minute?"

"Of course." I gesture for him to come in, and he closes the door behind him. "What can I do for you? Is everything okay?"

"I don't think my life could be any better," he says

with a small smile and shoves his hands into his pockets. "Except for one thing."

"And what's that?"

Vaughn licks his lips. "I want to ask your daughter to marry me."

And there it is, the kick to the stomach that I knew was coming. I know she's twenty-five, but Christ, it feels like we brought her home from the hospital last week.

"I know it's fast," he continues as if he has a sales pitch all worked out in his head. "But I know. I *know* there's no one else in the world for me."

I blow out a breath and nod. "She's incredible. I agree."

"She's the fucking *best*, and that's because of you and Natalie. I know that."

"I need to know that you'll protect her," I say to him. "From everything that this life can throw at her. Our world isn't always a kind one, kid, and I don't just mean Hollywood."

"I know," he says with a sober nod. "I'm already taking steps to back off on work a bit to make our lives as calm as possible, and she and I will work together to make sure we're both comfortable."

"She told me."

He nods again. "I knew she would. We'd like to sit down with you and Natalie, run some things by you."

"Our door is always open. What about when times

get hard?" I ask and sit on the edge of my desk. "When it's not all fun and sexy and easy?"

"It may be fun and sexy, but it hasn't been easy, let me tell you," he says with a chuckle. "Nothing worth having is easy, you know?"

Right answer.

"I know. No one will ever be good enough for her. And I don't mean that as an insult."

"And I don't take it as one," he replies. "I know I'm not good enough, but for reasons I can't put my finger on, she loves me. And I'd be a complete moron to let that slip through my grasp."

"You're no moron," I agree. "I'll give you my blessing if that's what you're after."

"Yeah, that's what I want. I'd like to ask her in Iceland, at Christmas."

The kid is a romantic. Good. She deserves that.

"I think that sounds nice."

Vaughn nods and then wipes his hand over his mouth. "Great. Thank you. I'll get out of your hair. But I want you to know, I'll not only take care of her, but she'll also never want for a thing. She'll have everything she needs and more, and I'm not just talking about money."

"If I thought you were, I'd have said no."

He smiles, licks his lips again, and nods.

"You're no moron, either."

"No. I'm not. Welcome to the family, Vaughn."

He shakes my hand and then pulls back, letting out a little laugh. "Fuck, I was nervous."

"Good. Now, go make your plans. I'm going home to my wife."

I haven't needed to see my girl this badly in a long, long time. And when I walk through the front door, I'm not disappointed.

There she is, with her computer in her lap, going through photos.

"Hey there, handsome," she says as I lean over to kiss her. "How was your day?"

"It ended interestingly," I reply and nudge the computer aside, then pull her into my lap. She cuddles in the way she's done for many years.

"What happened?"

"Vaughn came to visit me and asked if he could marry Livie."

"Oh." Her eyes fill with the tears I expected, and I pass her my handkerchief. "Shit, I knew it was coming, but it still slapped me in the face, you know?"

"Yeah, I know." I kiss her cheek. "How did this happen? She was a baby five minutes ago."

"I know." She swallows and wipes at the tears. "I like him so much. He reminds me of you. And if he's half the man you are, she'll be just fine."

"God, you still undo me," I whisper and bury my face in her neck.

"I just thought of something. Luke, I could be a grandmother soon."

That makes me grin, and I kiss her cheek again. "You're the hottest grandma I've ever seen."

"I'm not ready for that."

"We're not there yet. You just have to get ready for a wedding in the not-so-distant future."

"She'll be a gorgeous bride."

"How am I supposed to give her over to him?" I ask, voicing my biggest fear. "I know they're living together, but marriage is another thing entirely."

"You'll do it the way you do everything else," she says. "With kindness and class. And you'll trust our girl. Vaughn is a good man."

"Doesn't mean I won't worry."

"Are you kidding? We'll worry until we're dead. That's our job."

"I have plans for tonight," I inform her and watch as her green eyes darken.

"Oh? What's that?"

"Eventually, we'll make our way to the bedroom and get naked. But first, I have this."

I set a wrapped box on her knee.

"You and your gifts," she says, unwrapping the gift, and then shakes her head. "Jesus, Luke. This has to be ten karats."

"If you don't like it…"

"Take it and die."

I pull the ring out of the box and take her hand. I slip her old ring off and replace it with the new one.

"It was time for an upgrade. You've more than

earned it, not that you have to earn something like this."

"You spoil me."

I kiss her lips softly, breathing her in. "Always, baby. You know that."

She grins and hugs me close. "Let's get to the naked part."

"I thought you'd never ask."

ABOUT THE AUTHOR

Kristen Proby has published more than sixty titles, many of which have hit the USA Today, New York Times and Wall Street Journal Bestsellers lists.

Kristen and her husband, John, make their home in her hometown of Whitefish, Montana with their two cats and dog.

[f] facebook.com/booksbykristenproby
[o] instagram.com/kristenproby
[BB] bookbub.com/profile/kristen-proby
[g] goodreads.com/kristenproby

NEWSLETTER SIGN UP

I hope you enjoyed reading this story as much as I enjoyed writing it! For upcoming book news, be sure to join my newsletter! I promise I will only send you news-filled mail, and none of the spam. You can sign up here:

https://mailchi.mp/kristenproby.com/ newsletter-sign-up

ALSO BY KRISTEN PROBY:

Other Books by Kristen Proby

The With Me In Seattle Series

Come Away With Me
Under The Mistletoe With Me
Fight With Me
Play With Me
Rock With Me
Safe With Me
Tied With Me
Breathe With Me
Forever With Me
Stay With Me
Indulge With Me
Love With Me
Dance With Me

Dream With Me
You Belong With Me
Imagine With Me
Shine With Me
Escape With Me
Flirt With Me
Change With Me

Check out the full series here: https://www.
kristenprobyauthor.com/with-me-in-seattle

The Big Sky Universe

Love Under the Big Sky
Loving Cara
Seducing Lauren
Falling for Jillian
Saving Grace

The Big Sky
Charming Hannah
Kissing Jenna
Waiting for Willa
Soaring With Fallon

Big Sky Royal
Enchanting Sebastian
Enticing Liam
Taunting Callum

Heroes of Big Sky
Honor
Courage
Shelter

Check out the full Big Sky universe here: https://www.kristenprobyauthor.com/under-the-big-sky

Bayou Magic
Shadows
Spells
Serendipity

Check out the full series here: https://www.kristenprobyauthor.com/bayou-magic

The Romancing Manhattan Series

All the Way
All it Takes
After All

Check out the full series here: https://www.kristenprobyauthor.com/romancing-manhattan

The Boudreaux Series

Easy Love
Easy Charm

Easy Melody

Easy Kisses

Easy Magic

Easy Fortune

Easy Nights

Check out the full series here: https://www.
kristenprobyauthor.com/boudreaux

The Fusion Series

Listen to Me

Close to You

Blush for Me

The Beauty of Us

Savor You

Check out the full series here: https://www.
kristenprobyauthor.com/fusion

From 1001 Dark Nights

Easy With You

Easy For Keeps

No Reservations

Tempting Brooke

Wonder With Me

Shine With Me

Kristen Proby's Crossover Collection

Soaring with Fallon, A Big Sky Novel

Wicked Force: A Wicked Horse Vegas/Big Sky Novella
By Sawyer Bennett

All Stars Fall: A Seaside Pictures/Big Sky Novella
By Rachel Van Dyken

Hold On: A Play On/Big Sky Novella
By Samantha Young

Worth Fighting For: A Warrior Fight Club/Big Sky
Novella
By Laura Kaye

Crazy Imperfect Love: A Dirty Dicks/Big Sky Novella
By K.L. Grayson

Nothing Without You: A Forever Yours/Big Sky
Novella
By Monica Murphy

Check out the entire Crossover Collection here:
https://www.kristenprobyauthor.com/kristen-proby-
crossover-collection

Made in the USA
Middletown, DE
23 June 2022